TO DANCE THE BEG

To DANCE THE BEGINNING OF THE WORLD

STEVEN HAYWARD

STORIES

EXILE
editions
Fiction, Poetry, Translation, Drama and Nonfiction

Library and Archives Canada Cataloguing in Publication

Hayward, Steven, author
To dance the beginning of the world : stories / Steven Hayward.

Short stories.
Issued in print and electronic formats.
ISBN 978-1-55096-468-4 (pbk.).--ISBN 978-1-55096-471-4 (pdf).--
ISBN 978-1-55096-469-1 (epub).--ISBN 978-1-55096-470-7 (mobi)

I. Title.

PS8565.A984T6 2015   C813'.6   C2014-908423-4
                                C2014-908424-2

Text Design and Composition by Mishi Uroboros
Typeset in Fairfield and Trajan fonts at Moons of Jupiter Studios

Published by Exile Editions Ltd ~ www.ExileEditions.com
144483 Southgate Road 14-GD, Holstein, Ontario, N0G 2A0
Printed and Bound in Canada in 2015, by Imprimerie Gauvin

We gratefully acknowledge, for their support toward our publishing activities,
the Canada Council for the Arts, the Government of Canada through
the Canada Book Fund (CBF), the Ontario Arts Council,
and the Ontario Media Development Corporation.

Canadian Sales: The Canadian Manda Group, 664 Annette Street,
Toronto ON M6S 2C8 www.mandagroup.com 416 516 0911

North American and International Distribution, and U.S. Sales:
Independent Publishers Group, 814 North Franklin Street,
Chicago IL 60610 www.ipgbook.com toll free: 1 800 888 4741

For Katherine, Frances, Eddie, and Jimmy

THE AUTHENTIC: AN INTRODUCTION

I was at Wooglin's, the deli across the street from the college where I teach, when my mother called me on my cell. I'd just ordered breakfast and the truth is I didn't realize at first that it was *my* phone that was ringing because my children had, yet again, changed my ringtone.

This was something they found hilarious and, therefore, did all the time. In the last week my ringtone had been Prime Minster Trudeau saying something about how there was no place for the state in the bedrooms of the nation, Donald Duck singing "Deck the Halls," a crowing rooster, an improbably funky song in which the singer asks the rhetorical question about what would he turn "it" down for, and it was now a filet-o-fish commercial in which a speaker pleads with someone – perhaps the Mac-Donald's corporation itself – to give him that filet-o-fish, to give him that fish.

"Dude," the waiter told me, "that's *your* phone."

"So," my mother said, when I finally picked it up, "you *decided* to answer. You think I don't know how it works? I know how it works. It's the circle of life. You bring a child into the world. You feed him and clothe him, you nurture him, you drive him to soccer games and you go to his graduation. Later, he sees your name on his cell phone and he decides not to pick up."

"It doesn't work like that," I told her. "That's nothing like the way it works."

"Where are you?" she said. "I hear people. Are you out?"

"I'm having breakfast," I told her. "I just ordered."

"You ordered *already*?" she said. "What are you having?"

"I'm having breakfast," I said, loudly this time.

"I can *hear* you fine," she said. "What're you *eating*?"

"For breakfast?" I said.

"What do you think?" she said. "Yes, for breakfast."

I hesitated for a moment, then said I'd got the melon plate.

"*You* got the melon plate?"

I confirmed this was the case.

There was a moment of silence on her end. "Are you doing the dieting again?" she said.

"You don't say *the* dieting, Mom," I said. "You just say dieting."

"Now who's the English professor?" she said.

"I *am* an English professor," I said.

"Fine," she told me.

"It's my *job*," I heard myself say, lamely. "I do it for a living."

"Here you are, Professor Hayward," said the waiter. "One Authentic."

"This is what they call the melon plate?" said my mother. "What kind of breakfast place calls the melon plate The Authentic?"

It was not, in fact, a melon plate. The Authentic is a breakfast sandwich that consists of three eggs, three slices of bacon, three sausages, three different kinds of cheese, all sandwiched between two halves of a bagel and smothered in green chili. It was, in other words, exactly the kind of breakfast sandwich my doctor had recently suggested I not even *think* about, much less actually order. But ever since he had told me not to eat it, ever since my doctor sat me down to have that frank conversation in which he advised me to stick, strictly, to melon plates and nothing else, the urge to have The Authentic had become irresistible. I'd be standing there in the early morning, the sun not yet up, brushing my teeth, and the thought of it – of the cheese and the eggs, the sausages – would appear, unbidden and implacable. Most days I was able to resist. But not all of them. For writers, the short story is a like that. Some days you are able to resist. Not all of them.

Hence these stories.

After a decade – okay, fine, *two* decades – of writing and teaching short fiction, the temptation to begin a collection of short stories with something like a systematic statement about the form is almost irresistible. One stands before the reader, just as one has stood in front of his students, and feels the obligation to say something about the particular pull the short story continues to exert upon the literary imagination. But what is there to say? Short fiction is temptation. The literary equivalent of the breakfasts one's doctor – like one's agent – tells us to push out of our minds. There's no future in the short story. No money. If you want to live, there are a lot of good reasons to avoid short fiction. But most of us cannot.

Hence these stories.

For writers, the attraction of short fiction is plain enough. The short story offers a chance at perfection in a way that the novel doesn't. No matter how great the novel you write turns out, no matter how realized it is as a work of art, it retains something of the loose and baggy monster that it has to be, a half-made thing that drags behind it the reptilian tail of the book it might have been. A short story is nothing like that. It is a quick, bright thing. There is a perfection in such economy. A novel, on the other hand, is an ongoing relationship. As such, you worry about it. Even before you start writing it. Is this the novel for me, you ask yourself? Do I love this novel enough to write it? Are there other novels that I would love more? Am I making a mistake?

The short story prompts no such reservations. It's an assignation in a dark corner of the city, something that might very well go unnoticed. It means nothing. People read your short fiction and you shrug it off. It just happened, you hear yourself telling readers, it's not what it looks like.

As for the reader, however, I cannot but think that to the reader short fiction offers promise of complete immersion. This is something the novel cannot do. No matter how assiduous the reader, a novel necessarily involves the everyday – answering the phone, making dinner, checking your email, driving children to swimming practice. Short fiction, on the other hand, extends at least the promise of reading a thing from beginning to end without interruption. It cannot be an accident that so much short fiction – and the stories in this collection are no exception – take as their subject the interrupted, impetuous action. The unfinished, ill-considered act. A novel gives us a fully furnished fictional world, a wide lens through which to view the truth about things as they are. Short fiction harbors no such aspirations. It is a tale told around the fire, during which you dare not move lest you break the spell. Fiction is like a dream inasmuch as we do not want to be woken from it. In this way, the short story is the purest expression of the storytelling impulse.

That from which the rest of it springs. The authentic.

"What did you call me about anyway?" I asked my mother, who had not said anything for a long time. I wasn't sure she was still on the line and my breakfast would soon be cold.

"I'm sending you an email," she told me. "It's a picture of you." My phone made a little chirp and a moment later I'd opened it. "That's you," she told me. "I think you're six."

It *was* a picture of me. I had on a bright red cape, and in my right hand was a long metal pole which I appeared to be lifting up toward a darkening sky.

"What's in your hand?" my mother said. "It looks like a lightning rod."

"It's not a lightning rod," I told her. "Don't be ridiculous."

"Are you dancing?" she said. "You look like you're dancing."

"I don't know," I said. "I don't remember any of it."

"Look how cute you are," she said. "You were so cute."

Looking at the photograph, I had to admit that yes, in fact, I had been cute.

"You're *still* cute," she said. "And you're still my boy. Don't let anybody tell you any different."

And then she hung up.

But I kept looking at the picture. Of course I remembered. It was a lightning rod and it was summer. I remembered the red cape and the darkening sky. And the dancing. That was the year my father died, when I made up my mind to become a super-hero. I didn't know when or how it would happen, whether it would be a radioactive spider or gamma rays or if I was, in fact, a mutant possessed of unknown and remarkable abilities that had yet to reveal themselves. The lightning rod was part of that; it was unclear that being hit by lightning would lead to my gain-ing superpowers, but it was worth a try. The dancing, I figured, could not hurt. Sitting there in the diner I began to think that maybe it was just a matter of time. Maybe it was a matter of con-centration. I stared down at the breakfast I never should have ordered and willed myself to burst suddenly, incandescently, into flames. Nothing happened. Instead, I lifted The Authentic off the plate and took a bite. Most days I am able to resist. Not all of them.

Hence these stories.

STRAVA

Strava is a smart phone application invented by Michael Horvath and Mark Gainey, a pair of friends who were crewmates in college and missed competing with each other after they moved to different cities. Early in 2009, they realized GPS data had become specific enough to identify climbs based on elevation and distance and that it should be possible to record people's times and compare them. This is what Strava does. It tracks your movement. It tells you how fast and how far you ride and compares you to the rest of the world. You upload your data and it takes your measure.

The application launched in early 2010 and now has about ten million users worldwide. I am one of them. My name is Tim Babcock, and I'm forty-four years old. This puts me at the very edge of the thirty-five to forty-four age bracket on Strava. Twenty-nine days from now I'll turn forty-five and expect to see a consequent jump in my Strava ranking.

I am not, ordinarily, a competitive person. As a child I was the sort of kid who had his nose perpetually stuck in a book. I'm an English professor by profession. I do not play football or baseball. I am a poor swimmer. But who among us cannot be swept up in something larger than ourselves? Who among us does not want to win?

Strava was brought to my attention by my new physician, Smith Barnard. At the time, I was sitting on the edge of an examination table in my underwear, in his Colorado Springs office. It was my first appointment with him.

Colorado Springs is a city of a half million people built into the foothills of the Front Range, an hour south of Denver. The people who live here tend to be part of two distinct, though occasionally overlapping groups: they are either in the military or are ex-Olympic athletes. Smith Barnard belonged to both groups. He'd been a reserve on the 1992 Olympic volleyball team, and had spent two years training in Colorado Springs, at the Olympic Training Center in the center of the city.

Though Barnard went to Barcelona with the rest of the team, he did not actually get on the court. Nor did he even get into uniform, though he appeared briefly on national television, sitting in the stands in a patriotic sweatsuit, clapping in an encouraging way. This information is readily available. Anyone can view the videos on YouTube. I have not spent a lot of time watching those videos, but I have seen the evidence. Smith Barnard, no matter what he might say, is not an actual Olympic athlete.

When pressed, he'll assert that the fact that he didn't seen any actual volleyball action didn't bother him. He knew he was going to enlist and that, while enlisted, he was going to medical school. His army life lasted a decade, during which he was stationed at various bases around the United States, including Fort Carson in Colorado Springs. When he left the service he came back to the Springs where he planned to open a practice, get married, maybe have a couple of kids. Which is what happened, more or less, except for the getting married and having kids part. Meghan met him in Natural Grocers buying protein powder in bulk. I don't know exactly what was said but she came home telling me that she'd found me a doctor.

Meghan is my wife.

I had not entered Barnard's office that day with a specific complaint. The appointment had been made at Meghan insistence. She had become worried about my *inertia* – that's her word for it, not depression – and I appeased her by going for a physical. She had been impressed by Smith Barnard and said I should give him a chance. My current doctor didn't seem to be having much success improving my condition, she pointed out, and it was clear I needed to do something. The week before I'd come in to have my blood taken, and now Barnard had my file open in front of him.

It was not, I could tell, good news. In person, Barnard is imposing. Six foot four, square jawed, blue eyes, shaved head. With his white coat on, he looks like Mr. Clean, only cleaner.

"These are not good numbers," he told me.

I was unsurprised. I am the sort of person who has long ceased to possess good numbers and I am at peace with that. Once upon a time my numbers were okay, but even then my good numbers were of the temporary variety. I have a memory of my childhood pediatrician remarking to my mother that perhaps I should ease up on the waffles. Matters have not improved, but I have ceased to be cowed by the dismayed look that passes over a doctor's face – something involving the eyebrows, a sort of facial throwing up of the hands – when confronted by my medical records for the first time.

But Smith Barnard did something different. "See for yourself," he said, and held the file open for me to see.

I found myself staring at a chart delineating four categories: underweight, normal, obese, and morbidly obese.

I nodded gravely, though the chart made no sense to me.

"This is you," said Smith Barnard. His finger lay atop an oversized dot firmly in the middle of the quadrant labeled "morbidly obese."

Despite a lifetime of humiliation in doctors' offices, I was momentarily speechless. How does one gracefully respond to the news that one is morbidly obese? Is it appropriate to weep inconsolably? Fall on my knees and beg forgiveness?

I did neither; I argued the point. The process of arriving in morbid obesity, I observed, should be more gradual, more in keeping with the manner in which the weight had been accumulated: skinny, not so skinny, *not* skinny, perfect, *maybe* a little heavy, a *little* heavy, *heavy*, *quite* heavy, quite heavy *indeed*, obese, and then, a condition almost impossible to contemplate, *morbidly* obese.

I said this to Smith Barnard.

"Is that a joke?" he asked.

I confirmed it was a joke.

"I'm glad you can joke about this," he said.

I couldn't tell if he meant it or not.

"Give me your phone," he said. I unstuck my legs from the examination table and got down on the cold floor. The phone was in the front pocket of my pants. When I gave it to him he handed it back immediately. "Unlock it," he said.

I did as I was told.

"This is Strava," he said, banging away at the screen with his index finger.

I watched him install the application. When he was finished he handed the phone back to me, and there descended into the office an awkward silence which I recognized immediately as the same silence that descends at the end of Chekhov plays as the characters contemplate their impossible future. It is the sound of a way of life ending.

"It's not just about getting into shape," he said. "It's about getting moving. That's what you need right now. Motion."

"Were you ever actually in the Olympics?" I asked him.

"I was on the team, if that's what you mean," he said. "But we're talking about other things."

I nodded in the direction of a large photograph of him spiking the ball. "Is that a picture from the Olympics?" I asked him.

He closed my chart. Then he said: "You're going to love Strava, Meghan does."

I stared at him.

"It's all she talks about," he said, then laughed.

I laughed back, but the fact is that until that moment I'd never heard of Strava.

Carl ("Kip") Filmore was a forty-one-year-old project manager from Piedmont, California. He was married with two children, a steady job at Assurant Health, and was well liked by his friends and co-workers. He died suddenly after a gruesome cycling accident that occurred while he was descending a road near Mount Davidson in the San Francisco area. As awful as the accident was, the events leading up to it were unremarkable, even mundane. He hit the brakes with slightly too much force and lost control. Though it is difficult to know what exactly happened, police determined that he had not been hit by any car, nor had the crash been the result of some obstruction in the roadway. A car had pulled out and stopped. That was it. It distracted him momentarily, caused him to break a little too vigorously, and that was all it took.

According to Strava, Filmore was doing at least 20 miles above the 30-mph limit. Previous to that afternoon he had been the KOM record holder for that descent and, earlier that afternoon, had learned that someone had clocked a better time.

KOM stands for King of the Mountain. In Strava language it means that you're winning. Not the winner. There are no winners in Strava because the race does not end. Someone can always show up to unseat you. Clock a better time.

Strava is a Swedish word. It is a verb meaning "to strive."

After leaving Smith Barnard's office I considered going by the college, but thought better of it. I was still on a leave of absence and knew that my presence might be disconcerting to some. The details behind my decision to take a leave need not detain us here. Suffice it to say, I was under a great deal of stress and I do not respond well to stress.

Instead, I went home and dug my bike out of the back of the garage. It was a steel-framed ten-speed which lacked even toe clips. I couldn't remember the last time I'd ridden it. Miraculously, the tires inflated and the pedals turned. I decided to ride it to the park at the end of the street. Some part of me felt certain that Smith Barnard had installed Strava on my phone because he was sure I wouldn't use it. He'd sounded encouraging, like he was trying to help, but there was something about the way he pushed at my phone, prodded it with his index finger like he'd have preferred to knife into it, that made me think otherwise. The house Meghan and I live in is located halfway up a long hill. That means it takes about a minute to get to the park – it's downhill the whole way – and much longer to get back.

This is what it's like to own a bike in Colorado Springs. You're either going up or down a mountain. The fact is I couldn't make it home. Eventually I got off and walked my bike up the hill. When I got to the house I uploaded my data to Strava and it was then that I noticed that Smith Barnard had sent a request to "follow" me.

This is the verb. On Facebook you "friend" someone; on LinkedIn you "connect." Follow is what it is people on Strava do to one another.

As I stood there sweating in the driveway, it occurred to me that under normal circumstances, in any other year, I'd be about halfway through my Milton course, giving my lecture on the question of free will and predestination and the Miltonian understanding of it. Free will, I would be telling the students, is the ability to make a choice between two actions. You have the free will to choose to jump off a cliff or not. Once you make the choice to jump, you can't stop falling.

Meghan is a medic in the Canadian army stationed in Colorado Springs to look after the sizable Canadian contingent of soldiers stationed there because of NORAD. Actually, she's an obstetrician, but if you were to meet her – say in downtown Denver, say on the sixteenth floor of an upscale apartment building at a cocktail party that you've been dragged to by a colleague to celebrate the launch of a local poet's work – that is precisely how she would put it. She would say "medic," and then wait while her interlocutor got a faraway look in his eyes as he pictured her darting selflessly between foxholes, kneeling down in the dark, muddied earth, staring into the despairing eyes of a soldier.

"Really," I said. "A medic?"

"Actually," she said, "I catch babies."

Her tone was dismissive. I thought: this is what it's like when you are a soldier. Babies aren't born. They're caught. Then back to the battlefield.

"What's a medic like you doing at a poetry reading like this?"

"A girlfriend of mine is a girlfriend of the girl who copy-edited the book," she said. She held in her hand a glass of white wine. Stemless, untouched.

"I teach English," I said.

"So, you're a writer?" she said.

"I teach the Renaissance," I said. "There is a difference."

"Still," she said, "it's literary."

She raised the glass of wine to her lips and took a small sip.

Instead of a glass of wine, I realized that I held in my hand a paper plate stacked with cheese. The reason: I'd been standing in front of the cheese plate when it dawned on me that the colleague with whom I'd come that night was more interested in the mediocre local poet whose book was being launched than me. Of course she was somewhat younger than me, but I had believed, however foolishly, that a connection was possible. This realization was followed by a wave of dismay and it was then that my eyes alighted on the cheese.

Under normal circumstances – in a less fragile state – I would not be the sort of person who would ever do such a thing. But I was not quite myself. Meghan seemed to perceive this – to see something my colleague had not – and looked at the cheese on my plate for a long moment. I prepared myself for a negative reaction but it did not arrive. She winked, reaching out to take a single cube of cheddar, lifting it to her lips to take a single bite out of its corner. A discreet, tiny dent.

Then she replaced the piece of cheese on my plate. Her eyes were locked with mine the whole time. Without breaking my gaze, I took the cube she'd bitten into and swallowed it whole.

"You want to get out of here?" she said.

It was, simply, a very forward thing to say. I was taken aback. I have grown used to such things. That is Meghan. She moves quickly.

The next thing I knew we were out the hallway, in an embrace, but the elevator turned out to be broken. I pushed the button, then hit it again. Nothing. I was prepared to go back into the cocktail party, if only temporarily. The host would make a call and technicians would be dispatched. Meghan, however, was undeterred. "Catch me if you can," she said, and ran toward the exit sign at the end of the hall. She pushed the door open and ran down the stairs.

I sprinted after her, calling out for her to slow down. She did not. Below me I could hear her heels clicking against the concrete. I realized she was serious. If I didn't catch up to her – if I didn't catch her – before she reached the ground floor, she'd be out the door and I'd never see her again. Now, with real desperation, I quickened my pace – I was running, jumping down to and three sets of stairs at a time. I was gaining on her, I believed, though it was hard to tell. Meghan is fast. And thin. Looking at her undressed, what strikes you is the way the bones of her shoulders blades protrude upwards, as if they had at one point considered extending out into wings. She was a swimmer originally – 200m IM – but in her thirties she turned to triathlons. If we had been moving in the other direction, I would not have stood a chance. But gravity was on my side. I was gathering momentum, and by the time we rounded the corner on the third floor I could see the blond of her hair flashing, hear her laughing.

"Stop," I called out, winded. One floor remained. It dawned on me that I was not going to be able to catch her, and was about to give up when I tripped. I felt my left foot hit against my right calf and then, suddenly I was airborne. I flew by her, smashing into the exit sign above the doorway. The last thing I remember before the back of my head hit was the look on her face as I sailed by her. I'd beat her down; she was impressed.

She rode with me in the ambulance and we were married a couple of months later. It was good, for a while. For almost three years. Then she met Smith Barnard. I imagine they both had protein powder in their hands at the time, or else not quite yet. Perhaps they were both standing in front of the protein powder section, making the kind of obscure deliberations that one makes when buying protein powder.

Colorado Springs: city, so called, of champions.

Though most of the photographs of the horrific bike accident involving Carl ("Kip") Filmore have been suppressed by the family, there were witnesses, and many of them used their phones to photograph a scene that would soon become almost mythic. Filmore, it seems, after braking, went over the handlebars and skidding along the pavement. It was his face that hit the ground, and on which he skidded, for some 30 meters. This is how fast he was going, the velocity required to maintain his standing as KOM on Strava.

Doubtless, the gruesomeness of what happened is part of the reason why the incident has achieved such notoriety. It is hard to look at the photographs of the faceless, clearly screaming dead cyclist. All it took was an unlooked for car pulling out a little too suddenly. It could happen to me, you find yourself thinking. It could happen to anyone.

When Meghan arrived home from catching babies that evening she was surprised to learn about Smith Barnard putting Strava on my phone. She was pulling her biking shorts over her lean legs, and seemed confused about what exactly had happened.

"He made you give him your phone?" she said.

"He installed it *himself*."

"That's pushy," she said.

"*He's* pushy."

"He's intense." She didn't look at me. "It's part of his training, he's that person."

"Don't you think it's strange he's not married?" I said. "I mean, in his office there are no pictures. Not of anyone. Not even a girlfriend."

"Why would anyone put pictures of his girlfriend in an examination room?" she said. "I don't have a picture of you in my office."

"A guy like that?"

"What do you mean, a guy like that?"

"He's Ajax," I said. "Seriously."

"Ajax?"

I took a breath and started to explain but she raised a hand. "I'll get the footnote later," she said. Then she sighed. "Maybe he's just waiting for the right person."

"To catch up to him, you mean," I said.

Meghan was tying her shoes and said nothing.

"That was a Strava joke," I told her.

"Got it," she said. Now she was putting on her bike helmet.

"He's already following me," I said. "On Strava. He follows you, but you know that."

"He follows a lot of people," she said.

"Why didn't you say anything about it?"

"About Strava?" She gave me a frank look. "Why would I tell you anything about Strava? You haven't got off the couch in three months."

"I *have* a bike," I said. "I went for a ride today. Two miles, two hundred calories."

"The calories thing is always exaggerated," she said.

I told her about the ancient tires inflating. "Isn't that amazing?"

"It is," she said, though she had clearly stopped listening to me. The last thing she did before leaving the house was pick up her iPhone off the kitchen table and open Strava. "You're following me?"

"You have to accept it though," I said. "You have to agree to me following you."

"I know how it works," she said.

"Maybe we can go for a ride together some time," I said.

She tapped her phone. "There," she said. "Happy?"

Though it is does not appear in the pages of the *OED,* it is generally accepted that the word "gamification" makes its first appearance in the English language around the year 2002. Coined by a British computer programmer named Nick Pelling, who designed a number of early video games – including Invader and Hedgehog – it refers to the process of using game thinking and game process to solve problems and improve performance. If you think you're playing a game, you perform at a higher level than if you think you're working.

"Even if you have hundreds of friends on Facebook and you told them about your great ride today," Michael Horvath – one of Strava's creators – is quoted as saying "only a handful of them are going to care about it in the level you described. Strava gives you a way to really focus in on the friends in your life, the people that you are following, or the people that are following you, and to share this important part of your life with them."

After Meghan left the house, I opened up Strava and looked at her profile. Here is a list of the things I learned about my wife:

1. She owned *three* bikes: a "Focus Izalco Pro 2.0 (on which she had ridden 1,208.8 miles), a "Gary Fisher Hifi Deluxe 29er" (420 miles), and a "Stumpjumper FSR Comp" (233 miles).

2. She averages five rides a week, averaging 60 miles a week though often exceeding that.

3. Her longest climb was 1,345 feet.

4. She "and one other" scored a KOM on a section of road called Sunrise Decent.

5. Sunrise Descent is a stretch of road two miles long that Meghan ("and one other") had covered in just over two minute's time. This means she had been going almost 60 miles an hour.

6. As fast she had been going, the "one other" she was with had been going just a little faster. She seems to have eased up at the end, at the steepest part of the descent. He did not. If anything, he accelerated and, consequently, scored the KOM, not her.

7. The "one other" was Smith Barnard.

One of the many factors contributing to Strava's popularity is that it enables you to "track your effort" with precision. In addition to the duration of your ride, the distance covered, and the calories expended (however inflated), you can *also* track your "Energy Output" ("a factor of how much you're pedaling," says the Strava website, "how fast you're pedaling and how much force you're exerting on the pedals"), your Average Power ("Expressed in W," Strava will tell you, "a measure of how much energy you are placing into the pedals") and your "Suffer Score" which is an analysis of one's heart rate data. ("By tracking your heart rate through your workout and its level relative to your maximum heart rate," Strava says, "we attach a value to show exactly how hard you worked. The more time you spend going full gas and the longer your activity, the higher the score. The more time to spend coasting, or resting, the lower the score.")

In other words, if you stop pedaling – if for any reason you get off your bike – Strava knows. Looking at my own abortive rides, I could see clearly the moment when I gave up each time. When I failed to get up the mountain. As humbling as it was to see my inadequacy catalogued with such digital accuracy, my humiliation was tempered when I noted that Smith Barnard –

and Meghan – habitually did the same thing. Though capable of meteoring down Sunrise Descent, they almost invariably paused – sometimes for a significant interval – on the way up. This is the sort of data that Strava provides you with.

I will admit that I am no stranger to humiliation. Indeed, there is nothing easy about having been made to take a mandatory leave of absence. There are the endless hearings, the repetitions, the reiterations of who said what and the implications. By the end of the process a great relief descends. Much of that relief has to do simply with not having to tell the story any longer, to make any further admissions. A colleague, yes, and yes, there was a tenure process involved, a romantic attachment also, yes presumed, yes now in the past, and yes, I accept full responsibility.

And at some point one has to tell one's wife.

"What did you do?" said Meghan. This was a Friday. She'd just got back from a ride and was in the process of taking off her biking helmet. As usual, she was flushed.

"It just happened," I said.

"What happened?"

"The fact is," I said, "I don't know where to start."

"Start at the start," she said.

It might have been over then. I can see that now. Three months pass and she comes home from Natural Grocers. "I found you a new doctor," she will tell you.

"I'm fine," you tell her back.

"I'm worried about your inertia," she'll say. That's her word for it.

A key aspect of Strava's functionality is a mapping function which allows one to plan rides in advance and follow the rides of others. According to Strava, there are two routes that Meghan (now my ex) traveled, on bike, from our driveway to Sunrise

Descent. The first, less direct, less arduous route is a moderate ten and a half mile climb known as Gold Camp Road. The other is an almost impossible climb up Bonne Vista Drive. I had driven up it a couple of times – most recently with Meghan's parents (she had been driving) – to show them the views from the top of the Cheyenne Mountain. Though I labored mightily, I soon gave up and I thought to turn off Strava, but didn't. There was nothing to be ashamed of, I told myself, even Smith Barnard and Meghan had had to rest – often for a substantial interval.

Indeed, Strava showed me the approximate spot where the two of them tended to give up, in front of a sprawling, palatial home that looked down on the whole of Colorado Springs. A massive American flag flew in front of the house. It was a magnificent vista; I can see why they stopped, I remember thinking, at which point the garage door of the home began to move.

Thinking I had lingered too long, that it was the owner of the house, some Republican with a shotgun charging out to tell me to get off his property, I began to continue my arduous climb up the hill. But instead of an enraged landowner, out of the garage came a helmeted figure in blue and white cycling gear, a gleaming weightless road bike in tow.

"Don't worry," he said, satirically, as he mounted the bike, "it's all downhill from here."

It was then I recognized him. "Okay, Doc," I said.

"Tim?" said Smith Barnard. "Is that you? How'd you get up here?"

I gestured to my bike. "I was doing okay to begin with," I said. "But we all need to catch our breath somewhere. This is a popular spot."

If he made the connection, I didn't see it. He took off his sunglasses. "I'm impressed."

"You told me to change my life," I said, and gestured to my drenched T-shirt. "This is what that looks like."

"Good for you," he said.

Then we stood there for a moment.

"This is a big hill," I said. "I don't know how you guys do it. You and Meghan, I mean."

"Is that your bike," he said. "How old is that?"

I said I didn't know. "The tires inflated."

"No wonder you can't make it up this hill," he said. "You need a better bike. You know what, I'm going to give you one of mine."

"No need," I said.

"I insist," he said. "It's the least I can do."

"The least you can do?"

It took him a second. "For getting you on Strava," he said. "You wouldn't be here if not for me. I take full responsibility"

"Keep your bike," I told him.

"Look," he said. "I know you're not working."

Now it was my turn to nod and say nothing.

"Anyway," he said, and seemed about to say something else, but changed his mind. "I'll drop it by." And a moment later he was gone, pedaling with ease up the mountain. Watching him glide up the hill, I found myself wondering why he had needed to stop. Maybe, I found myself thinking, it was Meghan who'd had to stop that day.

I kept on pushing my bike uphill and at some point a blue blur, that I understood was Barnard, swished by me, shouting to me to keep going.

I got to the top forty minutes later, then coasted down to the bottom of Sunrise Descent.

"Coasted" is decidedly the wrong word for it. It was a downward descent that frightened me to death. You start at the top and plummet. As harrowing as the first two-thirds of the ride is, as steep a descent, it is nothing compared to the final third where there is a precipitous, numbing drop. When I arrived at the bottom I threw down my bike and vomited. It was hard to imagine what it would take to be King of the Mountain on such a stretch of road. But Smith Barnard had done it. Tucked himself into a sleek hurtling blur. He had done it.

When I got home, Smith Barnard's bike was waiting for me at the house, propped up against the front of the garage. Meghan pulled up shortly afterwards. Whether or not he had called her – warning her, I suppose – I don't know, though I expect so. These are the things that become part of the public record. They will come out at trial. Cell phone records. I expect to be a suspect. I also expect there will be no actual evidence.

Meghan saw Smith Barnard's bike in the driveway. "Is he here?" she asked, and I saw it in her face. She had imagined this scene. Practiced her reaction. It was just his bike, I told her, he'd given it to me. Then I watched her face change. If I didn't know before, I knew then.

The key point to make in the teaching of *Paradise Lost* is that Satan's escape from hell will never happen. Hell is not a physical location, you tell your students, it is a state of mind. He carries it with him.

I said nothing. Gave no indication whatsoever that anything had changed. That I had done the math. Uploaded the data. Seen the leader board. Not the next day and not the day after. On occasion, I would take the bike Smith Barnard had given me and ride it, allowing Strava to take my measure, though it became a somewhat more lonely endeavor.

Meghan told me she'd grown tired of it, being always in a race, and though Smith Barnard said he was planning to do the same, he didn't. Perhaps it had something to do with being the King of the Mountain. It is not something you let go of easily. On occasion I would see him whizz by me, a blue and white blur, poised in headlong descent.

Going at that speed, everything is a fine calculation. Anything can throw the rider off the biked. Over the handlebars and into the concrete. A rock in the roadway, a car pulling out unexpectedly, there is so little margin for error. This morning I got in my car and drove to the top of Sunrise Descent and floored it, all the way to the bottom.

Faster than humanly possible. I uploaded my ride. King of the Mountain.

Then I drove back up Sunrise Descent. Not to the very top, or even the middle, but to the bottom third. The steepest part where those descending it are nothing but speed and reflexes. The point of the descent where touching the breaks at all becomes a risky proposition.

I don't know exactly what happens when you lose your KOM. If it's an alarm that goes off, or if you get an email notification. Maybe both. Soon enough, Smith Barnard will find out.

It is only a matter of time. I'm keeping the engine running. It won't take much.

AUNT[1] DAISY'S[2] SECRET SAUCE[3] FOR HAMBURGERS

---

[1] Daisy was my great-aunt, the eldest sister of my paternal grandfather. She was born on November 17, 1916 and died on March 13, 2003 at the age of eighty-six. I found the recipe in her kitchen, on the back of an index card, nestled among yellowed newspaper clippings and unusable coupons. As her only living relative in Toronto who was not in the hospital with a broken hip, as her only niece, it fell to me to take charge of her possessions. I was her great-niece, that is, or lesser (depending on how you figure it).

[2] Aunt Daisy's full name was Daisy Frances Black, which she changed at the age of twenty-four, after marrying Paul McCartney – who was neither the bass guitar player of the Beatles nor the songwriting partner of John Lennon.

This other Paul McCartney, my Uncle Paul McCartney, was a tall, willowy man who drove the College Street streetcar for twenty-seven years. When his eyesight began to fail, he was put to work in the basement of the TTC headquarters at Dupont and Spadina sorting through the contents of streetcar fare boxes, the locked contraptions into which Toronto Transit passengers still deposit their tokens and cash when boarding. The thing to watch for, Paul McCartney used to tell me, were the rolled-up dollar bills; hundreds of times he had unrolled a dollar bill to find only half of it there and a note attached saying the TTC would get the other half on the way back. There was a room somewhere at the TTC Headquarters, he said, where such half dollars were kept. If you'd gotten the key and had the time, a pretty penny could be made.

I used to dream of that room, of getting in there with a roll of Scotch tape and of spreading the different ends of the different dollar bills around me, the way I did my father's dark banker socks, which were always impossible to match.

By the time I was born, Aunt Daisy and Paul McCartney had already moved out of their house on Palmerston and into a small two-bedroom apartment on Lawrence Avenue in the west end of Toronto, next door to the small two-bedroom apartment my grandfather and grandmother had occupied ever since they'd gotten rid of their house. Sunday mornings after mass, my father and I would drive out and have lunch there, with all four of them – my grandfather, grandmother, Aunt Daisy, and Paul McCartney.

So it was that I grew up thinking of my aunt and uncle as a second set of grandparents, spares who were ready to step in and take over if anything ever happened to the first set. I knew this to be a distinct possibility, for one of the stories Aunt Daisy told repeatedly was of how, once, she and Paul McCartney were riding the Bathurst bus when the driver passed out from heat exhaustion (it was the height of summer and they were on their way to the Canadian National Exhibition – the "Ex" as they called it – to buy a stickless frying pan at the Better Living Building).

They happened to be sitting near the front of the bus, and when the driver slumped forward onto the steering wheel, Paul McCartney stood up, removed the driver, and did what needed to be done. My sense of their being substitutes or grandparent equivalents (not exactly the *same*, that is, but not necessarily *worse*, the way that, in some recipes, particularly when it is fish you are cooking, you can use oregano instead of tarragon) was enhanced by the fact that both Aunt Daisy and Paul McCartney bore a physical resemblance to my grandparents. Where my grandfather was tall and willowy, so too was Paul McCartney; where Daisy was short and broad through the chest, so was my grandmother.

There was also the fact that my mother had died while giving birth to me, from what was described simply as complications. That is what the death certificate says exactly, in capital letters: COMPLICATIONS ARISING FROM CHILDBIRTH. So it was that my childhood was itself complicated, by the echo of impermanence, by multiple, seemingly interchangeable grandparents, and by a single father.

3 The idea of a "secret sauce," and, more specifically, of a secret sauce that could transform hamburgers, is, of course, a trademark of the McDonald's Corporation. As a child of the '60s I am old enough to remember a time when McDonald's was just one of many fast-food restaurants. This was something that changed in the 1970s, after the appearance of the Big Mac. Invented in 1967 by a Pennsylvanian named Jim Delligatti, the Big Mac combined extra-thin patties, special sauce, lettuce, cheese, pickles, onions, and a sesame seed bun. The result was a sandwich which sold wildly; McDonald's was pushed into the position of cultural ascendancy it still occupies today.

As difficult as it is to imagine in these days of carbohydrate paranoia – when it is not only possible to buy a sauceless Big Mac and a Big Mac made entirely of soy but also a Big Mac sold without lettuce, cheese, bun or anything else on it – at the time when the Big Mac first appeared, it was the special sauce that recommended it most forcefully, because the special sauce was the part of the sandwich that was impossible to make yourself. You might be able to get a sesame seed bun, you might be able to fashion yourself two extra-thin patties, but the special sauce was another thing entirely. The sauce was also made to seem more secret and more special by virtue of the extent and expense to which McDonald's went to guard the secret of what was in the sauce and how it was made.

I recall the newspapers reporting the efforts of the McDonald's Corporation to recover a cookbook they themselves had distributed to their managerial staff. This cookbook contained, among other things, the secret of the special sauce. Carefully photographed raids took place across North America, in which serious-looking young men in suits and dark sunglasses took back copies of the cookbook from apparently renegade, and sometimes just confused, managers.

Whether or not the raids were covert advertisements I cannot say. But if they were, they worked wonderfully, for the task of making one's own special sauce became a project to which thousands, if not hundreds of thousands of women applied themselves. Aunt Daisy was one of them, and she believed herself to have done a better job than most. So it was that hamburgers became our midday meal on Sundays when lunch was always made by Aunt Daisy, and always served in their apartment.

This apartment of theirs, then, was much as it is now: a brightly lit, yellow place where the air was still and warm. Paul McCartney would grill the patties outside on an old charcoal hibachi and drink beer with my father and grandfather. So it was that I first gained entrance into the secret world of women, the realm of those who knew how to make the secret sauce. Aunt Daisy would bring ingredients out of the fridge, carefully measuring them out, and I was in charge of the mixing. "No streaks, Martha," she would tell me, then hand over the spatula. Watching me the whole time.

Ingredients [4]

[4] The call informing me of Aunt Daisy's death came when I was at work. It was the most ordinary and workaday of circumstances; there was a message on the answering machine. I found out later that my father, who was laid up in the hospital with his hip, was the one who suggested calling me. Arrangements, the message said, would have to be made. Aunt Daisy was in the apartment on Lawrence when her heart finally gave out.

She was found in the kitchen, dropped there to the floor as if she'd turned herself into a drop – as if she'd known she was about to become something that would have to be cleaned up, and made her way to the surface where she would make the least mess.

The next day I went over and wondered how it was that I'd gotten involved in this business. What was I doing? What had I done? What are the things – the ingredients – that got me to this place, lost among a dead woman's pots and pans and old bedspreads? I knew the answers, of course: that, to begin with, it had nothing to do with me but that it began a long time before I was born in a town named Marmora in Northern Ontario on May 20, 1917 with the birth of my grandfather – not quite six months after the birth of my Aunt Daisy.

There were some, my father among them, who doubted that Aunt Daisy and my grandfather were actually born so close together. Daisy had the birth certificates to prove it, but even with the birth certificates, my father said he didn't know if it was true or not. He held that the whole idea of two babies being born six months apart was a fiction created either by a mistake that had been made long ago by the Ontario Provincial Government or by Aunt Daisy herself, who simply had believed the lies her parents had told her.

This was not something that came up often, but when it did, Daisy would produce the grainy black-and-white photograph of herself and my grandfather as infants. In the photograph Aunt Daisy is on her father's – my great-grandfather's – knee, a fat eight-month-old in a frilly white gown, perched there, balanced and weeping.

The occasion of the photograph would seem to be her baptism, but if you look closely enough (and you did have to look closely) you can see my grandfather, Daisy's younger brother, is in the photograph as well, curled up inside my great-grandfather's right hand which is tilted toward the camera, as if it contained not a baby at all but a tiny bird that he is putting back in its nest. The family had come the twenty miles to East Croydon where the nearest Catholic church was to get the two infants baptized at the same time. My grandfather had been born some four or five months premature, and no one had expected him to survive his first night, much less a whole month. But at the end of a month – this is all according to Daisy who (as my father always observed) was too young to remember any of it – my great-grandmother began to worry that the little baby had grown a soul, or, rather, that in not dying right away, the little thing had given them plenty of time to arrange for a baptism.

So my great-grandfather was forced to take them all into East Croydon and have all of it taken care of at once. That way, if the little thing died, it died. Whenever Aunt Daisy told the story, she tried to pass it off as nothing unusual – that people have always wanted to have pictures of their children taken and that this was as true in the summer of 1917, in Marmora, Ontario, as it was in downtown Toronto where people carried cameras around with them. But no one believed her, and on the occasions when Daisy brought out that old, faded photograph, there was always a queer silence as it was passed around, when you looked at it and wondered what had brought them into the photographer's studio that day.

$^1/_4$ cup Miracle Whip [5]

2 tbsp sweet relish, trained [6]

"There's a baby in that picture," my father would say. "But it's not your grandfather."
"Who is it then?" I'd ask him.

"One that got away," he would say, sounding every bit as Irish as my grandfather had ever sounded, despite the fact that neither of them had ever been outside Canada.

What my father thought was this: there had been a baby between my grandfather and my Aunt Daisy and that the photograph was of that lost, nameless baby who'd come so tiny into the world, and left so soon.

"You don't know that," Aunt Daisy would tell him.

"I know people," was always my father's reply.

My father worked as a loan officer for the Toronto Dominion Bank, which meant he spent his days trying to decide what people were worth and what they could pay.

"Do you ever get a feeling about someone," I sometimes asked him, "and just want to give them the money anyways?"

"No," he told me, and by the way he said it, I knew that he knew exactly what I was talking about. That it was a feeling he had all the time.

[5] There is little, if any, agreement between those who have sought to replicate the special sauce. There is no one recipe. Although the once widely held belief that the special sauce is *nothing* but Thousand Island dressing has been debunked, there remains a good deal of debate even about how to begin the sauce. Some say Thousand Island dressing. Others say French dressing (orange, not red) and some, like Aunt Daisy, say Miracle Whip. Upon closer examination of Daisy's recipe box, I see this is not surprising in the least, for Aunt Daisy used Miracle Whip whenever possible, and, indeed, often when it was unnecessary. Aunt Daisy, it seems to me now, did not decide upon the ingredients in her recipes strictly on the basis of taste. She appeared to like the *idea* of Miracle Whip.

[6] Although I know this to be a spelling mistake, that what Aunt Daisy meant to write was "drained," the idea of differentiating between trained and untrained relish strikes me as something Aunt Daisy would do. She was the sort of woman who seemed to have taken hold of herself at some indeterminable previous moment, and thereafter refused to let go. It was something for which she was admired the older she got. She knew this, of course, and once told me that not weeping at funerals was the chief virtue an older woman could have. She certainly practiced it, particularly at her husband's funeral, which occurred some fifteen years before her own.

Paul McCartney died one August afternoon in the supermarket parking lot after having a massive coronary as the result of lifting a heavy bag of Macintosh apples into the trunk of their car. Aunt Daisy had already sat herself in the passenger seat, and did not know what had happened until she got out of the car. The first thing she saw, she said, were the apples rolling down the black pavement in a haphazard, frightening way, like blood-coloured ribbon. Then she saw Paul McCartney and knelt down, trying frantically to bring him back. When she found she couldn't, she closed his eyes herself, lay down beside him on the warm parking lot pavement, and waited for the ambulance to arrive.

Sugar and Salt [7]

[7] In the immediate aftermath of Paul McCartney's death, a number of initiatives were taken to keep Aunt Daisy active. There was talk of theatre ticket subscriptions and walking tours, support groups and cooking classes, but Aunt Daisy had her own ideas, of course, and in the summer of 1976 she insisted on taking me to the Olympics, which were being held in Montreal that year. Bruce Jenner would win the decathlon and Nadia Comaneci – who was exactly the same age as myself, a kind of accusation levelled at fourteen-year-old girls everywhere – would score the first ever perfect ten in Olympics gymnastic competition. Pierre Trudeau, who was Prime Minister at the time, would try to prevent Taiwan from marching in the opening ceremonies and several African nations would walk out because New Zealand had sent a rugby team to tour white supremacist South Africa.

Aunt Daisy caught Olympic fever before any of that happened. She'd seen the advertisements on the television, taken down the address, and written away. Two weeks later the glossy brochures from the Canadian Olympic Committee detailing cost and ticket availability had arrived. She had never been much of a sports fan, but she felt, like hundreds of thousands of other Canadians, that it was her duty to attend the games. It also seemed to Aunt Daisy to be a sound investment; the construction of the Olympic stadium had cost one and a half billion dollars and she, as a taxpayer, had already invested considerably in the event. This trip was remarkable in and of itself, but was more remarkable given that Aunt Daisy had never been to Montreal. The single great trip of her life occurred some fifty-four years earlier when she was eleven and my grandfather was eleven (it was June) and my great-grandfather decided that it was time to move himself and his family out of Marmora. The circumstances under which this conclusion was reached are shrouded in mystery, but it seems to have had to do with a foreclosure and a broken jaw.

Whatever the case may be, my great-grandparents moved themselves and their children into the upper floor of a tiny house on Bourne Avenue near Dufferin Street, north of Bloor. It was 1928, the year before the Depression began, and the difficulty of those years took its place in our family mythology. I would hear it all a thousand times: about the whole of the family sleeping together in a single bedroom; about my grandfather, out with his snow shovel, being turned back at Yonge Street by the police because he was a Catholic and the east side of the city was Protestant in those different days; about how Aunt Daisy and my grandfather had stood for hours outside of Honest Ed's at Bathurst and Bloor to get a free turkey. I knew less about my father's growing up, which had included playing hockey at St. Michael's alongside the fabled Phil Esposito. On the mantle of the fireplace in the house on Westhumber where I grew up in west Toronto, there sat a picture of my father, at seventeen, with closely cropped hair, dressed in a dark suit, with a hockey bag in his hand. Saturday nights, which was one of the only times when my father was around the house, he would watch the Leafs play, pointing out the players he knew.

Why did he not remarry? I wondered that, but not overly. The same way that I wondered about whether he blamed me for my mother's death or if he secretly wished he were not a loan officer at all but a man among men, skating on the ice before the entire country. They were things that crossed my mind, but were not much more than footnotes to our story. Like footnotes, you could look too closely at them, or linger among them too long and get lost.

1 tbsp mustard powder blended with 1 1/4 tsp cider vinegar [8]

Mix thoughtfully [9]

DO NOT put in bleeder [10]

Add more Miracle Whip, as desired.

---

[8] Out of the blue one Sunday when Aunt Daisy was making the hamburgers, she spread out the glossy Olympic brochures on the white Arborite table in front of me.

"Are you going?" I said.

"Don't you think we should?" she asked me.

"We?" I said, and looked at my grandmother.

"Don't look at me," she told me.

"I know we don't have to," said Aunt Daisy. "But don't you think it's something we'll regret later if we don't?"

I opened up one of the brochures. Aunt Daisy was not really asking my opinion, of course; she had already decided that going to the Olympics was, absolutely, the right thing to do. As she told me later, after we had already bought our tickets and were on the Via Rail train, she'd decided it would be foolish to not go to the Olympics. Worse than foolish. It would be proud. It would be tempting fate.

"Fate?" I said. "Nothing's going to happen to you."

"It's not me I'm worried about," she said.

So it was that we went and witnessed Sugar Ray Leonard win his gold medal, as a way to keep fate appeased. It did not work. When we got off the train at Union Station my father was there to meet us. My grandfather had died, he told us.

"Where's Katherine," Aunt Daisy asked, referring to my grandmother.

"At the house," he said.

Aunt Daisy nodded, and we walked quickly to the car. Daisy stared straight ahead the whole way out to the apartment on Lawrence, and from looking at her you'd never have known that she was anything but tired from coming home after a long trip.

[9] I have decided this sentence is *not* a message to me. When I first picked up the recipe card that day in Aunt Daisy's kitchen, there was a moment when I thought the opposite. That Daisy had somehow foreseen it all. Her own death, that my father would be in the hospital with a broken hip – all of it, and that she had sat down and rewritten the recipe as a kind of message, a secret transmission. But that was for just a moment, for standing there it all came back to me and most particularly the way that Aunt Daisy mixed. There was nothing thoughtful about it. Sunday morning when the men were out grilling the meat, she would take the bowl out of my hands and put her shoulder into it.

"No streaks, Martha," she would tell me. "The secret of the secret sauce is to make people think it has never been anything but sauce."

[10] Every kitchen should come equipped with a blender. The sort of appliance into which you could simply stick a part of yourself – your hand, your finger, or something more dispensable like your heart – and be done with it.

But that is not the way things happen. Not for any of us.

The thing unfurls over time: we lose a part of ourselves, and another, and then another, and still another, and soon we find ourselves staring at a recipe card in a kitchen. But even that, even the recipe card, is a monstrous image, magnified, absurd, and certainly Aunt Daisy – whose death was a still drop, a simple, quiet plopping down in a kitchen – would not have it. No, I thought, no blender here. Not in this kitchen.

Of course I made the arrangements. All care had been taken, the notice in the *Globe* and the *Star*, and no expense had been spared.

There had been a planned visitation at the funeral parlour where white letters on a blackboard directed any and all to the smaller chamber in the back where Aunt Daisy had been laid out. But there had been only myself to look at her, rouged as she had never been in her life, her sore and scrubbed hands folded atop her.

Standing there, there were things I remembered, stories she'd told me so many times that it seemed like they'd happened to me: that it was I who had stood with my grandfather outside Honest Ed's to get the turkey, I who had kissed Paul McCartney for the first time on the observation deck of the Bank of Commerce building while looking down on King Street from the thirty-second floor. And later, after we have given up trying to have children of our own, that I was there when we drove down to the shores of Lake Ontario one summer night and turned on the headlights of our car so that they shone into the lake because we knew that, somewhere in the dark distance, a seventeen-year-old girl named Marilyn Bell was swimming towards us, a Canadian, one of us, the first woman to have ever swum to Toronto, all the way from Buffalo.

"Miss Black," said a voice.

I turned, and saw it was the director of the funeral home. "You've done a wonderful job," I told him. "She looks wonderful."

"Like herself, you mean?"

I paused. "No," I told him. "I shouldn't say that."

BEE GIRL

I'm Tallulah, the new Bee Girl at Lake Farm Park in Painesville, Ohio.

I throw in the Ohio because it's what you do when you're from Ohio. Watch the next time you see a kid from Ohio on TV. She'll come out with it. Like there'd be some confusion. Like anyone cares. She'll also maybe say "USA" but that's understandable. It's one thing to come from the country that basically conquered the world; it's another to come from some nowhere place in the middle of that country. Which is probably why she comes out with it in the first place. If you're from Ohio, you know the last thing you expect to see on TV is someone from Ohio. Except Halle Berry. Or Jerry Springer. But they don't count. What I'm talking about is ordinary Ohio people who have no business on television. It isn't so bad, I suppose, when you think about it like that: the Ohio girl's taking up a few seconds of her few seconds on TV to tell someone else in Ohio she has a chance. To not give up, not just yet.

It was my father who got me the Bee Girl job, in a manner of speaking. He's best friends with Fred Travers, the director of Lake Farm Park. They've known each other for most of their lives, going to grade school and then high school and then to Ohio State together. Then they both got jobs at Riverside High – my father in the English Department and Fred Travers in the Geography Department – and about ten years after that, Lake Farm Park made Fred Travers an offer and he left teaching. They stayed good friends, which is why Mr. Travers was over at our house the day he offered me the job. He'd heard, as I suppose the rest of Painesville, Ohio, had, about my father telling the school board he wouldn't be coming back. They didn't ask why because they didn't have to. Everyone knew he had become a kind of basket case since my mother's funeral. Specifically, he had turned into the kind of basket case who's incapable of doing anything besides watch television. Fred Travers, I suppose, had come over to ask what the hell was going on or maybe to try to cheer him up and maybe both. At any rate, by the time I was getting home, taking the groceries out of the trunk of our Honda Civic and trying not to think about my mother, Fred Travers had given up trying to say anything and now was just sitting in the living room with my father, watching television.

When he saw me he smiled a weak smile that said he had tried to talk to my father, failed, and given up. I smiled back my own weak smile, which said I know what you mean. After a little while Mr. Travers got up and came into the kitchen to talk to me, asking when I'd be going back to school in Columbus. I said I hadn't made up my mind but that I'd probably stay around for a while. He told me if I was ever looking for a job I should come to see him.

I guess I was expected to decline, but I didn't.

"Good," he told me. "Come by tomorrow."

I told him I would.

"It's the least I can do," he said, and when he did he looked a little sick, as if it were not an expression anyone might say, but a statement of fact. As if there were more he could do but had decided not to. We went in to tell my father, who nodded in a kind of noncommittal way, like he'd just been told it was a national holiday in a country far away and that the banks were closed. Then he turned up the volume and Mr. Travers said he had to be going. By the tone of his voice, I could tell he was a bit offended, a bit impatient with my father, and that he thought my father turning up the volume was rude, a way of tuning him out when he had just done something good. It turned out my father – who even if he is a basket case isn't the kind of basket case that doesn't know what's going on around him – knew this as well, because he extended his hand to Fred Travers in an awkwardly conciliatory manner. "Thanks, Fred," he said, "for everything." They shook hands, and then my father turned back to the television.

The next day I went to Lake Farm Park and knocked on the door to Mr. Travers' office. He gave me some forms to fill out, and when I'd finished he handed me a green vest with LAKE FARM PARK written on the front of it in ornate gold script. Under the words there were embroidered golden pine trees and the embroidered roof of a barn which was also gold.

"You're the new Bee Girl," he told me.

I didn't know what to say to this.

"Is that all right?"

"I guess – I don't know anything about bees."

He waved his hands like someone cleaning a window. "There's no real bees anymore, anyway," he said. "Too dangerous, I say. The job, more or less, involves you putting together a little talk about bees and beekeeping."

I said I thought I'd be up for that.

"The talk is on the schedule for today," he told me, and handed me a list of the day's events, a copy of the schedule that is printed up each day by the old ladies who work at the front desk. "But they put it on every day, so don't worry about it. If anyone comes out and wants to learn about bees, just say you're new, and that they should come back in a week, when you'll have put together your talk. Or else tell them to ask

Chuck – he's our Tomato Guy – and Chuck can answer any questions."

The schedule was printed on one half of a piece of ordinary paper that had been ripped in two. This is what it said:

In the Visitor Center
Ice Cream Making: 11:00, 2:00
The Dairy Parlor:
Hands on Milking: 10:30, 11:30, 1:30
Machine Milking: 4:15
Cheese making: 10:00, 3:00

Lake Farm Park Gift Shop:
Farm Park honey and maple syrup.

In the Arena
Meet the Horse: 11:00
Light horse demonstration: 2:30

Well Bred Shed
Eggs, eggs, eggs: 10:30, 12:15
Sheep herding: 10:30, 12:30, 3:30

The Barnyard
See some of our many farm animals.

Plant Science Center
The Great Tomato Works: 11:00
What's buzzing with bees: 2:30

"All set?" he asked. It was a way of ending our conversation. "All set," I said, and thanked him again for giving me the job.

"It's the least I can do," he said again, in just the same way that he had said it the day before, in our kitchen. Then, after a beat, as if he had stopped being my boss and was now Fred Travers, "How's your father, I mean, really?"

"It's hard to say."

"What does he do, besides watch television?"

"Sometimes he orders pizza."

Mr. Travers shook his head. "He looks a wreck, a complete wreck." I shrugged and raised my eyebrows, which was a way of saying that in the first place I knew nothing about the human heart, and, second, that even if I did, the heart under discussion was my father's heart, the emotional equivalent of his underwear drawer. Mr. Travers got the message. "Well," he said. "This'll get you out of the house at least."

"And," I said, "money."

It took him a minute to realize that I was joking, but when he did, he laughed and laughed, as if the laughter had been coiled up inside of him and waiting for a chance to escape. By this time I was used to it. That's one of the things about everyone knowing that your mother's just died. If you make any kind of a joke, anything that's even remotely funny, the rest of the world will just kill themselves laughing. I suppose this is because most of the time they're standing there worried you'll burst into tears, or get into some details they don't want to know, or say that you're going to kill yourself. Then, if you make a joke, all of that worry comes out all at once, as a laugh.

If you're like most people, you've never been to Lake County, Ohio, which is about an hour east of Cleveland. Lake Farm Park itself is located near the western borders of the county, on what is the outskirts of Kirtland, Ohio, but is actually much closer to Painesville, Ohio. Like it matters. The Farm Park is basically a farm that people are allowed to visit;

it was a farm that Lake County bought and turned it into a place where the kids in Lake County could learn about farm life. It's not really a tourist attraction despite there being a gift shop and a cafeteria and an information desk; it's more like a place run by farmers that will help them turn their kids into farmers. I've never known anyone who isn't from Lake County to visit it, although occasionally someone will drive east out of Cleveland, but they don't count – they're from Ohio. The Farm Park is set up like a semicircle: the Visitor Center is at the easternmost point, then there's a curving path leading to the Barnyard, the Well Bred Shed and, eventually, to the Plant Science Center, which is where the Bee Exhibit is housed. That first day, the Plant Science Center was empty, except for Chuck.

"You must be the new Bee Girl," he said. It was not a question.

"You must be the Tomato Guy," I replied.

It seemed for a moment that we should shake hands but Chuck stood there and nodded. You could tell just by looking at Chuck that he wasn't the kind of guy who was into shaking hands at all. He was old – I found out later he was twenty-seven – with shaggy red hair and a scruffy furry red beard and tiny freckled hands. Like me, Chuck had on a green Lake Farm Park vest, but under it he wore a tie-dyed T-shirt and very worn blue jeans with big white patches with doves on the knees. He seemed a bit shy because he couldn't quite look at me. Instead, he nodded toward the greenhouse. "Most of the time," he told me, "I'm in there."

"And I'll be in there," I said, "with the bees."

"You know there's no real bees, right?"

"Mr. Travers told me – too dangerous."

Chuck snorted. "Dangerous," he said, and shook his head.

Just so there would be no misunderstanding later, I said, "Travers went to school with my dad, which is why I got the job."

"Good for you," he said.

"I'm supposed to learn some kind of talk about bees."

"Don't worry," said Chuck. "Nobody ever comes all the way out here." He was a little bitter about it. "They hired a guy a few months ago, but he stopped showing up after a couple of weeks because he thought they wouldn't notice, so they had to fire him."

"So they *did* notice?"

Chuck shrugged. "He was an asshole. I came back one day and found him throwing tomatoes against the wall outside."

"So you got him fired?"

Chuck didn't nod but didn't look away either; he was warning me.

"So what's this bee speech I have to do supposed to be like?" I asked.

This seemed to disappoint him. "This isn't Disney World, you know," he told me. "It's not a speech – it's more like a class."

"I don't know anything about bees. I mean, what did the old Bee Girl do?"

"You can learn," he said, ignoring my question about the old Bee Girl. "There's a bunch of bee books in there, so don't worry – you don't have to go to the library or anything."

"Don't worry," I told him, in an unbelievably lame way, "I've been to the library plenty of times."

"I bet you have," he said, which was even more lame. Then he looked at me. "Have I seen you around somewhere?"

I told him I doubted it.

"No, I have," he said. "Are you the little sister of somebody?"

"Only child."

"Is Tallulah your real name?" He was looking at my name tag. "Or, like, an alias?"

"It's real," I told him. "It was my mother's name and before it was her name it was the name of a movie star. My grandmother named my mother after a movie star."

"I didn't know that happened back then," he said, and laughed. "I didn't know grandmothers named their kids after movie stars."

"Can I ask you a question?" I said then, because the way he was laughing made me angry and I was getting a little sick of him. "Are you a Billy Joel fan?" He didn't look like a Billy Joel fan, but for the whole of our conversation Billy Joel's *Glass Houses* had been blasting in his greenhouse, as if he'd been running around putting plant food in all of his little soilless pots and singing along to "It's Still Rock and Roll to Me" when I'd come in and forgot to shut it off. I knew he was shy about it because he pretended for a moment not to know what I was talking about, saying that maybe it had been on the radio and he hadn't noticed.

"What," I said, "the whole of *Glass Houses*?" The album was still on, but now Billy was singing about riding his motorcycle in the rain and telling dirty jokes.

"Now who's the Billy Joel fan?" he said, to get me back.

"It was my grandmother's favorite album," I said sarcastically. "My great-grandparents listened to it all the time when she was a baby." As lame a comeback as it was, I felt a little bad because Chuck had been caught red-handed and suddenly looked it. He hung his head in a kind of helpless way, like a villain at the end of a *Scooby-Doo* episode, out-smarted despite his best efforts. Like someone who had been convinced, again, he would never rule the world. Under his pretend-hippie beard he was really just a kid that never stopped liking Billy Joel when he was supposed to. I wanted to tell him that I was lying about it being my grand-mother's favorite album. That it had been my mother's, and that walking in and hearing it playing made me think that a ghostly version of her was maybe going to show up in the bee room and give me a message. But I also knew she wouldn't be there — which made me feel as sick to my stomach as had the thought of having to talk with some ghostly version of her. But I couldn't just say that, if I didn't want to seem as much as a total basket case as my father. Instead, I sort of smiled at Chuck and told him I wanted to get going on my bee talk. He said he had work to do himself and went into his greenhouse and turned the Billy Joel down, though not off. That he didn't turn it off completely made me like him then, a little. I started to think that maybe there was a future for the two of us.

When I got home I told my father about my day. He was sit-ting in front of the television, just as he had been the day before with Fred Travers. "I'm the new Bee Girl," I told him. "I have to teach a class about bees."

"Well," he said, "that won't BEE easy."

"That's a STINGER," I told him.

"Maybe, HONEY," he said, "you can get some time off for good BEE-HAVIOUR."

Then we both laughed and, just for a moment, he looked at me. Even if he were a basket case, I told myself, he was still my dad, the same person he had always been. "So what did you do today?"

"I was watching," he told me. "What else could I be doing?"

"What were you watching?"

He shook his head, like it was an absurd question. "I'll give you a clue," he told me, smiling, like he had just hit on a good line. "It's not behind the chair." Then he started switching chan-nels.

"What're you looking for?"

"Nothing," he said. "There's nothing on."

"Where's the TV guide?"

"That's useless," he told me.

"Just decide on something."

"I'm trying," he said.

"What are you looking for?" I asked again.

He seemed not to hear me. Finally, he stopped at 19 ACTION NEWS, which was just beginning. It seemed to relax him a little, the news coming on. But not really. It both was and wasn't what he wanted to see. I knew there was something, some sound bite, something coming in through the television that he wanted to show me, some story on the news that we were both trapped in. This was what we had to do, he seemed to be telling me to get things straight. To get things started. We needed the facts, the new news. And the sign that we were both trapped, wound up in some pre-recorded piece of old footage, was that his lines were always the same. So what I said – whether or not I was or wasn't the new Bee Girl at Lake Farm Park – seemed equally repetitious. There was something triumphant about his dismay at not seeing what he wanted to see, that he knew what he was looking for – at the same time as he knew it wouldn't be – on television. But at the same time, there was no alternative to switching channels, nowhere else for either of us to go.

For the next week I sat at the desk in the Bee Classroom with the bee books spread out in front of me, earmarking pages, high-lighting passages. Drawing and re-drawing outlines. The Bee Classroom was very like an actual classroom, only with these rustic imitation wood benches instead of desks. It had been designed to give the visitors the feeling of what it'd be like to learn about bees in an old-fashioned one-room schoolhouse, where they only taught students about bees. At the front of the room, where in a real classroom there would have been a pull-down map or a movie screen, there was a diagram indicating the different parts of a bee and another showing the inner workings of a hive. There was also a great deal of bee paraphernalia: jars half-filled with honey, an old wooden hive, that kind of thing — along with a number of colorful catalogues.

I found the catalogues were weirdest of all, because they were bee catalogues, each with a bright 1-800 number on the front that you could use to get bees sent to you overnight and a number of glossy photos showing how the bees would look when they arrived. Bees were sold by the pound, I found out, and a three-pound box contained about ten thousand bees; it was like buying a hive without a home, complete with a queen, the requisite number of workers, a few drones, and a can of syrup to feed on during their journey. The queen was confined to her own small cage at the top of the package. And in the pictures showing the arrival of the bees into their new homes and the happy people opening the boxes, the workers were always all clustered around the queen at the top of the cage. Without a home to defend, the catalogues promised, without any organization whatsoever, these bored bees could be moved easily into any waiting hive. Most of the time, while I told myself I was working, what I was really doing was listening to Chuck on the other side of the Plant Science Center: him rummaging around, going and coming back from getting whatever tomato supplies he needed, singing along to Billy Joel.

But then I discovered the Bee Garage.

Near the back of the building, the Bee Garage had been the center of the bee exhibit back in the days when there had been real bees; it was filled with the remnants of a medium-sized honey-collecting operation. There were four complete wooden hives and a number of cracked hive stands. There was a smoker and a feeder and a pair of white overalls, complete with a veil and helmet, lying in a kind of evacuated way in the middle of the floor as if the person inside them had just dissolved suddenly. Looking at those overalls made me feel a little like a survivor in one of those sci-fi movies who wakes up in a city where a neutron bomb – the kind of bomb that destroys all of the people but none of their things – had gone off, and it occurred to me that what hardly ever made it into those movies was the fact that all the clothes would be left over as well. Those movies just showed you the cars and money and the televisions – which would always be on and filled with channel-less static, a real sign that anything that had been before the bomb wasn't any more. I imagined those kind of bombs left behind a lot of things that probably no one wants to talk about and certainly wouldn't be any good in any movie: the gold in teeth, the braces of teenage girls, the artificial hearts of old people, their fake legs and wigs. If there were ever a real neutron bomb that went off, all of that stuff would be there as well, and surviving it wouldn't be the picnic those movies always make it seem like. If you were walking anywhere at all, you'd have to step over all that dead junk. Recognizing this as a morbid thought, as exactly the kind of thought that several professionals had told me to stay away from, I made up my mind to put it out of my mind altogether and convinced myself that I should instead feel like an archaeologist, picking my way through a lost city that had been buried a hundred years before. Soon it seemed to me as if everything had been pushed into the garage in what looked to be a rushed, careless way, as if the bee operation were the type of destroyed city that had known it would be destroyed – that someone had pulled it inside to get it out of the rain or away from the lava, or because meteors were battering the side of the earth. And that the old Bee Girl, the one who had been trying to save all of the bees and all of the bee stuff, hadn't made it herself.

At around noon, Chuck and I ate lunch together outside on the green lawn in front of his greenhouse. We could see it was a busy day for the interesting parts of Lake Farm Park: the sheepdog rushed around in the Shepherd's Field and mothers lifted their babies to pet the lambs. We saw a horse trotting, then cantering, then galloping; we saw a cow being led into an outdoors stall and then children one by one stepping up to milk it.

"Have you ever milked a cow?" I asked Chuck.

"Sure I have," said Chuck. "I used to work in the Well Bred Shed." He told me he'd worked at the Farm Park for eight years. "I *started* there," he told me. "Being the Tomato Guy is a promotion."

We watched a sheepdog barrel down a hillside, turning the sheep all in a single direction.

"Look at that dog go," I said.

"You know those dogs that herd the sheep," he told me, "they just know how to do it, the way you and me are born ready to stand."

"Maybe you were," I said. "I had to learn to walk."

"Actually," he told me, in a way that made me realize I was about to become the beneficiary of an interesting bit of trivia Chuck had bestowed on others before me, "for the first forty-eight hours of your life you *could* stand. No one knows why it's the case and it goes away after – but in that first day, you can stand up, as if you aren't a baby at all." I said that was very interesting, and Chuck went on. "That's the thing, though, not *all* the sheepdogs can do it – some of them lack the herding instinct. You put them into a pasture and they don't do anything." He looked at me then as if he was trying to make some big point that he hadn't thought all the way through, and that he didn't know if I'd get even if he had thought it all the way through. I sat there and looked back at him all the same, wanting him to make his point, looking at his shaggy red hair and wondering if that hair went all around him, if under his clothes was nothing but red hair.

"What's your favorite Billy Joel song?" I said suddenly.

"Well," he said quickly, as if it was a question he had frequently asked himself. "I guess I'd have to say 'Uptown Girl.'"

"No way," I said.

"What?"

"Are you kidding me?"

"What's wrong with 'Uptown Girl?'"

I shook my head.

"Have you heard it? I mean, have you ever really listened to it?"

"Everybody's heard it."

"Come on," he said, and I followed him into the greenhouse. Under one of the tables, in a box marked FERTILIZER that had a number of massive skulls and bones on it as if it were full of poison, he had every Billy Joel album, including *Greatest Hits* on CD, which he told me later he really didn't need because he had all the songs already but had bought it because it was like a mix tape of Billy Joel that Billy Joel had made for himself. While I waited for him to get the disc out and put it on, I noticed that he had somewhat dolled himself up. Instead of his tie-dye he was wearing a clean white short-sleeve shirt under his green vest. Then he put on the song and we talked about the video in which Billy Joel is a mechanic who romances a fancy girl who brings in a fancy car; part of the fun of the video, he told me, is that the fancy girl is Christie Brinkley who Billy Joel

39

actually married, which makes it seem that he wrote the song before they met, that it was the song that was responsible for their getting together.

"It's not that bad," I said, when he shut it off. "It's a good song."

"I told you."

"Mine would have to be 'The Ballad of Billy the Kid' – which is off *Piano Man*."

It was a statement to which I had put considerable thought while I should have been putting considerable thought into writing my Bee Speech. It had a predictable affect on Chuck; he was impressed. "You really know your Billy Joel," he said. Then he looked at me very closely. "You know," he said, "you're pretty."

"Not as pretty as the old Bee Girl," I said. I don't know why I said it, but there was something about the way that Chuck had not answered my question about her the day before that made me want to say it, made me want to bring her up again.

"She *was* pretty," he said after a moment "but not TV pretty – not the kind of pretty that makes you stop what you're doing and watch someone on TV, even if they're on for just a second or two."

Which was, approximately, when I realized he had remembered where he had seen me before. It wasn't the first time something like that had happened, not by a long shot, but having it sneak up on me like that was something new. I wanted to ask him how long he had known. Or else I wanted to just shrug it off, say it was a charming thing to say, and go on with my life. But, instead, I found myself just staring back at him, willing my features into motionlessness.

"That's you, right?" he said. "The girl whose mother was kidnapped?"

That stopped me. "Not kidnapped," I told him. "Killed."

"Killed?" he said, and then before he could stop himself. "Yes, that's right."

"Of course it's right," I snapped. Chuck looked down. "They thought she was kidnapped at first, which was why I was on TV."

If you're reading this anywhere in Ohio, you probably know the story. You probably even know what I look like. You know how my mother got up on a Tuesday and went to a dentist appointment but never made it into the ReMax office where she's an agent. At about ten, they left a message at our house asking if everything was all right, which my father didn't get until he'd come home from school. By the time he did get home there were a number of messages from her clients and also from the office. This was a couple of weeks after Christmas and I was still home from school. Those were the days when my father could do anything, and when he heard those messages he got on the phone right away to the cops, who came over themselves and told us personally that there was nothing we could do. Not for the moment. People sometimes take a drive for a day or so, and then they come back. Like it's a game. A way of spicing up their life. Both of us tried telling them my mother wasn't that kind of person. See if she isn't, said the officer, and I think it was supposed to be a good thing.

But then Tuesday turned into Wednesday, and then Wednesday turned into Thursday and still she was nowhere to be seen. By that point the police were taking it seriously, and had put out an alert for our Honda Civic, which she had been driving. They were also watching my father very carefully. I could tell that most of the policemen had made up their mind he was responsible for whatever had happened to her and were just sort of waiting around for him to confess it. They had to give up on that, though, after it became apparent that he had been teaching the whole time – and that nearly everyone at Riverside High was ready to say so in court. Before long, the police had started telling my father it was something like abduction and that maybe he'd get a ransom call. So he stayed by the phone and kept the television on in case there was some late-breaking news. I sat with him and the two of us sat by the phone, waiting for a call, and during that time my father talked about what he thought had happened to my mother. He seemed resolved on the fact that my mother *was* playing a kind of game with him, an adult version of hide-and-seek. That it was a kind of trick. She had run off to a place where he couldn't keep an eye on her, and that it was just a matter of time before we heard from her – the way that, when you're a kid if it takes you too long to be found, you help out the person who's it. Soon it was Thursday again, and one of the sergeants working on our case said they thought one of us should go on television and say something, that sometimes that sort of thing makes a difference. My father agreed to do it and the two of us went into the 19 ACTION NEWS studio and when it came time to tape the segment, he looked straight into the camera and said he didn't care if my mother came back or not. As if he were the one playing the game. The one making the rules. One of the sergeants working on the case came in and talked to him and said they were fairly sure something had happened, that whatever it was, it wasn't my mother's fault. My father said he understood, but when the cameras turned on again, he said very firmly that he was done looking for her. As if all the police, the television studio and all of the cameras and all of the people in it, were part of the game – something that had been foreseen and planned by my mother. My father, everyone realized, had become the kind of basket

case who refuses to believe that something h
wife.

Which is how I ended up on television.

"I'm Tallulah," I told the camera, "from Paine

They'd given me a picture of my mother, a b
that had been taken a few weeks before, at my
wedding in Brecksville, and in the real picture my
are also in the photo. I'm wearing a white dress a
mother, and my father is wearing a dark suit, looking
able because of the collar, which is too tight. "My h
only part of me that could escape," he'd said, just as th
was being taken, and my mother and I had laughed
earnest, wide laugh. The picture I held up was cropped a
could still see the dress she'd been wearing that day, and sl
has that smile, but my father and I are gone. The police
blown-up the picture so that the camera could pick it up ea
which made it look life-size, and when I held it up next to
own face I thought for a moment that my mother might st
talking to me.

And then I began to cry. That was as far as I got: the word
"Ohio." It aired that night. The next day we went back to the studio and I tried again, and again it was the same thing. Again, they
put it on. "I'm Tallulah," I said. "From Painesville, Ohio." And
that was it.

Like it made a difference.

A week later they found her. She had stopped by the roadside
to help a man who had shot her dead for her money and credit
cards. He had driven her car off the road and hidden it. They'd
got him somewhere outside of Ashtabula, drunk in a bar after he
started using her credit card. The whole time I'd been crying on
19 ACTION NEWS, she was already dead. Stuffed into the
trunk of our Civic, like a bag of groceries.

"So that's the story," I told Chuck. He nodded and said he was ry. "What's that?" I said, to change the subject, and pointed to arge green tub in the corner of the room.

"It's corn," he said. "Hydroponic corn – as far as I know, no ne's ever tried it before. That's corn that's been grown without he benefit of soil."

"Maybe soon you'll be the Corn Guy – or the Corn and Tomato Guy."

"Maybe," he said, as if it might be a real possibility, the kind of thing that would be entirely okay with him.

When I got home that night, my father was still in front of the television, almost as if he hadn't moved since I'd left that morning. He'd started with the television during the time when he thought my mother was still coming home, and then it didn't seem like he could stop. At first no one had noticed because he'd taken bereavement leave, which he'd extended, and because during the summer he didn't have to teach anyway, everyone thought he was getting over it, pulling himself together. But it was more than that. The television was on, day and night. He got up out of his chair only to go to the bathroom. When he was hungry he picked up the phone and would order pizza, leaving the front door ajar so that the delivery guy could bring the food right in, as if he was in the middle of his favourite program and didn't want to miss a minute. I knew something was up right away, though, because my father was never one for television. But in those first weeks I thought it was important to show my support, so I spent as much time as I could right there in the chair next to him. He would watch all kinds of things, from *Thomas the Train* to *Three's Company* reruns to *Alias* to late-night horror movies. One of the good things about my being the new Bee Girl was that I had things to tell him, new things. And that

night, because I felt like I'd made some steps forward in the Chuck department, I sat down next to him and told him about Chuck. "He's the Tomato Guy, right now," I said. "But he's working on being the Corn Guy."

"That's amazing," he said.

I told him I thought it was.

"No," he said. "A-MAIZE-ing – as in maize, which is to say corn."

"I think I might be in love with him," I said.

"Don't be so CORN-y," he told me.

Then, because I was feeling really magnanimous, I stayed there and we watched a movie called *Leaving Las Vegas* which is about a guy who loses his wife and loses his job and then drives out to Las Vegas in a convertible where he's made up his mind to get so drunk he dies. There's a lot of other stuff in the middle – he falls in love, which is nice and makes his dying not such an entirely negative thing – but in the end he dies: he drinks and drinks and then he's dead.

"Now that," said my father when it was over, "was a good movie."

It occurred to me he might be talking about himself. "It won't kill you, you know," I told him. "All this television."

He started changing channels.

"Did you hear what I said?" I got up out of my chair and stood between him and the television.

"Don't worry," he said. "No one's trying to kill himself."

"Then what?" I said. "What is it?"

Instead of answering me, he just sort of leaned to one side, so he could see. There were other things I wanted to say, but the way he looked around me made me not want to.

"Never mind," I said, and sat back down in my chair, and a little while later he asked me if I wanted to order pizza.

45

I told him he should do what he wanted, so he picked up the phone and dialed Domino's and the delivery guy came in about forty minutes later. He was a skinny guy, a kid really, but you could tell it wasn't the first time he'd been to our house because he made a kind of lame show of knocking on the front door and then walked straight in and put the pizza down in front of my father. I suppose they had a kind of arrangement because my father nodded to the kid and the kid nodded back, half-looking at the television and half-looking at my father – but not with disdain or pity or anything like that, but with respect, as if my father was doing the kind of thing that he had thought about a lot but had never done, like that guy in that Las Vegas movie who kills himself in a nightmare that's kind of a dream for everyone else but him.

I found the poem the next day. I was still getting nowhere with my speech, so I wandered in the bee garage where I picked up the white beekeeper's hat and put it on, pulling the fine white mesh veil down over my face. I suppose that I wanted Chuck to come in and see me and laugh and maybe to tell me that, if you looked at the mesh and the hat in a certain way while certain girls had it on, it looked a lot like a bridal veil. I waited for a while, but this didn't happen so I took off the hat and when I did a tiny white piece of paper fell out if it, fluttering down to the floor. This is what it said:

I ask them to take a poem
And hold it up to the light
Like a color slide
Or press an ear against its hive.

I won't lie: it was scary. It seemed to have been stuck up inside the hat so it would stay there until someone put it on. What was more strange was that it seemed to have been written to *me* by someone who had been able to imagine that one day I would show up, the new Bee Girl, and would be sure to put the hat on. So I took it and showed it to Chuck.

"It's a poem," he told me.

"Christie?" I said.

"The old Bee Girl," he said.

"It's kind of all right."

"It is all right, but it's not by her – it's not even a whole poem."

"What do you mean?"

"I mean it's about the first third of a poem by a poet named Billy Collins. In fact, he's the Poet Laureate of the United States."

"I didn't even know it had a poet."

"Well, it does."

"She had it stuck up inside the bee keeper helmet. What happened to her?"

Before he could say anything, there was the sound of footsteps on the gravel walk leading up to the Plant Science Center. Chuck and I looked at each other, thinking that maybe it was our first visitor – that someone had finally decided to make the long walk in order to find out what was buzzing with the bees. But then the door opened, and we saw it was only Mr. Travers. He said hello to the two of us and asked how everything was going. I said everything was fine, and then so did Chuck, who told him hello in a cold, formal way, asking him if he could spare a minute to come and look at his hydroponic corn. "Grown," he told Mr. Travers in a weirdly pointed way, "without the benefit of soil."

Mr. Travers knew he had no choice; he followed Chuck into the greenhouse.

Feeling it was important to look like I was taking the job seriously, I went in the bee classroom and tried to look like I was

47

cleaning up the place. I was pretending to dust off a large straw cone in the corner, picking it up and shaking it with a kind of intent businesslike look on my face, but before long I found myself looking at that poem again, thinking I'd have hated it had it been anywhere else other than that bee room. Now that I knew it wasn't a Bee Girl who'd written it – that it was really a poem about poems and not about bees – it seemed to me the kind of thing my father used to love to quote to his English classes in the days before he became a basket case. A poem written by an old man who thinks he's better than his students because he's forgotten what it's like to sit in the back of a class and know that at the end of the semester there's an essay you have to write. Looking at it that way, I started to hate it; I imagined the rest of the poem going on about how bad students are and how they are always wanting to do something terrible, the wrong terrible things, to poems – and thought it was good that the old Bee Girl only wrote out those first four lines. Maybe she hadn't made it up, but she had written it out. And when she did, she'd made it hers. It seemed to me what she liked was the idea of taking the poem and pressing it to your ear like a hive. Whoever wrote the poem was probably thinking he was talking to a bunch of bored students in a boring class and thought that comparing the poem to a hive was a dangerous and mysterious thing to do. But the poem is different when you read it standing in a garage filled with beekeeping paraphernalia; when you read the poem there you feel that the poem isn't about poetry at all, but about bees, and that makes you want to pick up an actual hive and hold it to your ear. Which is what I guess it was doing in the helmet.

"So, Tallulah, how are you getting on?" It was Mr. Travers. I had no idea how long he'd been standing there.

"Fine," I said in an overly jolly way, as if I'd been caught red-handed, "nothing to complain about."

"If you like, I could move you somewhere else, like to the cow exhibit."

"I like it here."

"It would be no trouble."

I assured him that I didn't want to go work with the cows.

"I'm glad to hear that," he said. He held up a cob of Chuck's hydroponic corn, and seemed stuck for a moment for something to say. "How's your father doing?"

"Pretty much the same."

"I suppose it's to be expected."

"Do you?" I said. It was a real question. I asked and then stopped myself.

"I mean, after all that's happened." I looked down, like someone really put in a spot. Which was entirely how I felt. "I had best be going," he said. Then he looked down at the corncob in his hand, which was really much smaller than a cob of corn that had been rooted in the ground and was a strangely bright yellow colour, like something painted instead of grown. "Would you give this to him for me?" he said, and handed me the cob. Then he went out the front door of the Plant Science Center, walking slowly down the gravel path.

A few minutes later, Chuck came in. He seemed about to say something but stopped when he saw his corn. "He gave it to you?"

"He gave it to me for my father," I told him.

"Does your father like corn?"

"No more than anybody," I said. "But this is really good corn."

Chuck was surprised by the compliment but also pleased by it, which he showed by scratching the back of his neck and then thrusting his hands into his pockets. I saw then that the poem was still in my hand, and that he had been looking at it. And had decided not to say anything about it. "Well," he said, as if he were officially bringing our meeting to an end, and turned around and left.

When I got home I gave the corn to my father. "Mr. Travers sent you this," I told him, dropping it in his lap so he would have to take his hand off the remote in order to place it on the table next to him. "He sent it, but Chuck grew it."

"Ah-ha," said my father.

"He's really nice, Chuck is," I said.

"Are you still in love with him?"

I shrugged, in the way Chuck shrugged all the time, as if to say it didn't matter to me personally one way or another.

My father nodded, seemed to be casting about for something to say, and then gave up when it didn't come. For a while I sat beside him, staring not at the television but at the little bright corn, and I began to feel sorry for the fact that it had come into the world without the benefit of soil, which in turn made me feel very sorry for myself and my father, and I began thinking of my mother as a kind of soil in which we'd been rooted and that we were both now like that little weird corn. For a moment it seemed like an important and profound thing to be thinking, and then it just seemed stupid, like something you'd laugh about when you're stoned but seems sad the next day. So, because there was nothing more depressing than sitting next to my father while he stared listlessly at the television, I got up and went upstairs and lay down on my bed. Determined to think about something other than my father for a change, I occupied myself instead by making a list of all the boys with whom I'd been romantically involved. The list looked like this:

Alex Roberts, 16 (kissed)
Scott Sclmull, 17 (kissed, lips)
Josh Olmstead, 17 (kissed, lips)

Adam Johnson, 18 (kissed)

Jason Dotson, 20 (kissed, lips; hand job)

Once I'd finished writing it, I realized it was not the kind of checkered past I'd imagined I'd have by the time I was twenty. Even with the hand job that I'd given Jason Dotson in the Painesville Cinema nine months previous during a showing of *Gigli* while Jennifer Lopez was doing calisthenics on the silver screen, my past was hardly checkered in the least. Still, I was determined to make the best of it, so I tried to bring back that moment, to recall the shy but businesslike way in which Jason Dotson had unzipped his fly while remaining in a sitting position, taken my hand in his as if he was going to walk with me down the aisle, and instead guided it over to his open pants while he stared straight ahead, at Jennifer Lopez. But then I found myself thinking of Chuck and that I'd never kissed anyone with so much hair on his face, wondering if I'd have trouble finding his mouth.

The next week I finally finished my speech about the bees. I boiled it down to four points, each of which had a kind of funny bit attached to it. Then I wrote each of the four points and each of the four jokes down on its own cue card:

CARD#1

There are twenty thousand different kinds of bees in the world and only ten percent of them are honey bees. Bees aren't wasps and wasps aren't flies and most of the time when a person says: "Ugh, a bee," it's not a bee at all. *Apis mellifera* the western honey bee.

CARD#2

Introducing the Queen, she's the mother of all the workers and all the drones and any other Queens the hive might raise. She's the biggest bee in the hive with a long, tapering abdomen like a super-model, her wings are short and her legs have no pollen baskets and she has no wax glands for the production of wax. What she does have is a stinger, which she uses mostly for stinging other queen bees; reports of queens stinging people are virtually non-existent. She lives for two to three years and lays two thousand eggs a day, every day for two or three yeas. All that and still has killer abs.

CARD#3

Introducing the worker bee: all the workers are girls, who wear out their little bodies with all the work they do and they die early most of the time. They don't reproduce like the queen, but sometimes, under very unusual circumstances, they do, and the result is a bunch of drones – male bees – that can't move or fly or do any-thing at all. Like most guys from Ohio.

CARD#4

The drones are all men. All they care about is mating with the queen, which is done so high up in the air that hardly anyone has actually seen it. The drone does no work and isn't equipped to work, with no wax glands and no pollen baskets and no stinger, and most of the time they don't see the outside of the hive and don't do much of anything. Which is another thing that makes them like most of the guys in Ohio.

It wasn't anything particularly insightful or maybe even that interesting, but all the same it was done. I was pretty pleased with myself and – probably because I wanted to impress him – I got the idea that I would put on the bee keeper suit and go in and try out the talk with Chuck. He was in the greenhouse, pouring water with the Billy Joel turned way up, and that was why he didn't know I was there until I tapped him on the shoulder. He turned around, looked at me once, and fainted. He was out cold and he looked like he wasn't breathing.

When someone is knocked out cold on TV, it's one thing. In the first place, everyone knows what to do. In the second place, you expect it. There's nothing strange about seeing someone knocked out in a TV show. People get knocked out on TV shows about as frequently as they go to the bathroom in real life. When it really happens, when all of a sudden you find yourself looking at Chuck on his back on the floor of his greenhouse, it's a different thing altogether. I suppose what I should have done is called 911, but instead I got down on my hands and knees and gave him mouth-to-mouth.

Which, as it turned out, did the trick.

I breathed into him a single time, and he opened his eyes. "God," he said, "my head is killing me." I got him up into a chair and brought him a glass of water. He drank it, and then he drank down a couple of Tylenols and I turned down the Billy Joel. After a little while he was looking a lot more like himself.

"I'm really sorry," I told him.

Chuck shrugged. "I wasn't expecting it at all."

Then it was my turn to shrug. "Sorry, anyway."

"Thanks," he said, "for bringing me back to life and all."

"Anytime," I said.

"Watch out," he said, "I might just take you up on that."

"I dare you," I said, and didn't move.

He walked across the room and kissed me, very firmly, like something he was determined to do. After that, we sort of retreated to our different corners. But we soon came out again. I walked into the greenhouse, and there he was.

"Chuck," I said, "tell me about the old Bee Girl."

"Who, Christie?"

"Were you friends?"

"You could say that."

"What was she like?"

"I don't know, she was OK."

"And?" I said.

"And what?"

"And what else?"

"She had brown hair – you mean that kind of thing."

"That's a place to start."

"Brown hair, about your height, blue eyes – when she laughed it sounded like she was throwing up." He did an imitation. "She was really into bees," he said, after a bit.

"What happened to her?"

"She left."

"Did she quit, or did you get her fired, like that other guy?"

"That other guy was an asshole."

"So, she wasn't."

"No, Christie wasn't."

I nodded and watched a little girl riding a pony in the distance.

"It was a temporary thing, working here," he said. "One day, she decided that was it and took off. And then after that, not long after it, the bees left too."

"Just like that?"

"It sometimes happens, though Travers was pretty convinced that she'd come back and taken them."

"That she stole the bees?"

"It would be easy enough, I suppose. Christie knew what she was doing when it came to bees. You'd just have to isolate the queen and the rest'd follow. People do it every day."

"How old was she?"

"What I'm saying is I don't know the details. But maybe she had something going with Mr. Travers."

I looked at him.

"Look," he said. "I know that he's your father's best friend or something, so I better just shut up."

"How old was she?"

Chuck shrugged. "Not old," he said. "But older than you." Then he smiled to himself. "About as old as me."

"Was she pretty?"

He didn't say anything for a moment. "Sure," he said next, in a weird abrupt way, "she was pretty." Then, as if he had just looked the word up in the dictionary, said, "Yes, definitely pretty."

"Do you have a picture?" I asked.

"No," he said very quickly. "No, not anymore." Chuck seemed to be considering this and looked very much like he wanted to shrug one of his fake shrugs but couldn't quite do it. "It's an old story," he said. "We were together before she worked here. I got her the interview, for God's sake." He laughed. "With Travers."

"She must have been pretty, then," I said. "For you to get rid of the pictures."

"I suppose I don't really know the details," he said. "One day she quit and that was it. A few days after that, the bees took off. The hives sat out there for about a week and then Travers came in and dragged them all into the garage by himself."

"And that's why there's no real bees anymore – it's got nothing to do with them being dangerous, does it?"

Chuck didn't know how to answer the question. "Anyway," he said, "she was pretty."

When I got home my father was watching *Thomas the Train*, which is a cartoon for kids about a bunch of engines, all of whom have different attitude problems. I tried telling him about the four types of bees, a version of my bee talk. "I'd start by asking them about honey," I told him. "And when was the last time they had it. Then I talk about the queen." He didn't seem interested in the least. In the episode of *Thomas the Train* that he was watching, Henry – a large green socially maladjusted, and very vain engine with an exceedingly deep voice – gets a new paint job and refuses to go out on a run because the rain will make his new paint run off. Everyone pulls him, then everyone pushes him, and when he still will not move they brick up the tunnel where he has stopped in order to get out of the rain, then lift up the old track.

"Haven't you seen this one?" I asked; I knew he had because we had watched it together, in those first weeks.

"Yes," he said, and I couldn't tell if he was looking at the television or past it, out at the stunted maple on our front lawn, as steadfast as the window itself.

I made spaghetti and meatballs for dinner and brought a bowl out to him.

"Thank you," he said, giving me just the briefest of looks.

He was watching the news.

"You know," I said during a commercial for Tide, "that she's not coming back. That there's not going to be some special bulletin telling us that she's alive and well."

"I know," he said. "Still, I'll keep looking."

"No one can look everywhere," I told him.

He looked at me then. "I give up," he told me, like we were playing a game.

"I give up too," I said.

After that, it seemed we should be able to resume our lives, our ordinary life in the room could continue. Except that my father would not leave his chair. Or turn off the television.

"They're not calling," I told him. "They're not *going* to call."

But it was like he didn't hear me.

Soon I gave up on talking to him and went upstairs. I took the phone number out of my pocket that I'd been carrying around for some time and dialed it. When I woke up the next morning I found him sitting in that chair, where I'd left him, sound asleep, the night before. The volume was turned down but the set was still on, and I took the pair of clippers that I'd borrowed from Chuck and cut the cable at the back of the television, picked up my purse and was about to leave through the front door when I put the purse back down, went back to the television, and cut the power cord as well. Then I called the 1-800 number and ordered him the bees and went out the door to work. I don't know if it was the right thing to do, but by now it is too late. The way I see it, he is the one who's not playing the game right, by making me so impatient that I don't know what I'm impatient for, or even know if I care whether or not he gets out of his chair. Whether it will take one day or two, I don't know, but sooner or later the bees will arrive. That he will call Mr. Travers, I don't doubt. I see him holding the package of bees on his lap and try- ing to think what he and they will do. I see him rising out of his chair and walking outside, getting behind the wheel. Then he will come here. Chuck has already helped me drag the old hives out into the big field. Mr. Travers will object, I suppose at the sight of them. It is the least he can do. It is only a matter of time before the disturbed hive, without motivation and with nothing to defend, makes its way to where it's supposed to be.

BUDDHA STEVENS

It was not until I attended the University of Toronto that I became aware of the fact that there was a poet named Wallace Stevens. Like all accounting students, I was required to take a humanities course as a breadth requirement. One afternoon in the second term, the professor directed us to read a poem entitled "The Emperor of Ice Cream" by Wallace Stevens. I was very impressed. But not by the poem – by the name of the poet. It was the first time I realized the name Wallace Stevens belonged to anyone other than the boy who lived across the street from me as a child. Today he is known as Buddha Stevens, and although it is perhaps difficult to believe, there was a time when he was not famous.

My name is Paul Bunce and I am employed as an auditor by Revenue Canada. I mention these details for their own sake. As an auditor, I am a man habituated to detail, and it is detail which interests me most. My purpose in writing is to supply certain neglected details in the biography of Buddha Stevens. I will be briefly discussing the famous Melvin Henderson Incident, as well as, of course, providing an accounting of my own recently publicized involvement with Buddha Stevens.

I should perhaps begin by stating outright that I have always been skeptical about Stevens' abilities. Doubtless, he possesses a certain talent, but I hold that this talent is somewhat limited, and that belief in any of his utterances should be qualified in the extreme. The fact that I have known Stevens since we were both very young affords me a unique vantage point from which to survey his personal development. Certainly there have been – and will continue to be – those who contend I have merely a personal score to settle with him. To my detractors, I can only reiterate the fact that my skepticism towards Stevens is less a result of my past association with him, and is more symptomatic of a general, personal exactitude which I extend to all matters.

Buddha Stevens and I were born in Ballentine Hill, a small town in northern Ontario. Ballentine Hill exists mainly because Yonge Street, the longest street in the world, runs through the middle of it. Its town hall, its church, its supermarket, its high school, its post office, its laundromat, and its police station are all clustered – like boats along the edges of a great river – within a one-mile radius of the famous street. This is the centre of town, and in 1976, when we were both sixteen years old, it was the centre of the world for Stevens and myself.

We lived in identical houses across the street from each other, and both attended Ballentine Hill High School. There were two different routes we could take when we walked home from school: the short and the long. The short route was the most direct, but it was unexciting. It took us past a parking lot, Reginald MacLillop Public School (which Stevens and I had both attended until we were thirteen), and a number of abandoned shacks. The long route, in favorable contrast, took us past the apartment where Bernadette MacLean lived.

When Bernadette happened to be walking home at the same time we were, Stevens and I would walk with her. But even when she was not with us, we'd usually take the long route. On those days, we would stand outside her apartment and look up at her window. We knew which window belonged to her because she had pointed it out for us on several occasions. It was on the third floor, and from the street we could see in it a large spider plant and a grey venetian blind. I have no idea what Stevens and I expected to see while looking up at her window but I doubt it was anything overtly sexual. I know I would have been content if she had peeked out from behind the blind and waved, acknowledging my chivalric presence on the sidewalk.

"I think Bernadette likes you," Stevens said to me, one afternoon while we were standing outside of her apartment. "Why don't you ask her out?"

I had been kneeling on the ground, tying my shoe, and I looked up at him with what must have been a surprised expression on my face. I had just been asking myself the same question.

"You think she likes me?" I asked him.

"I think so," Stevens told me.

"No shit?" I asked.

"No shit," he replied. (I apologize for this profanity, but I am attempting to deliver as accurate an account of these events as is possible, and this was the way we spoke to one another: people were either shitheads, full of shit, or getting the shit kicked out of them.)

"How do you know?"

"I just know," he said. "You should ask her out."

It may sound incredible today, when thousands of people worldwide make the most important decisions in their lives based upon a single ambiguously worded phrase uttered by Buddha Stevens, but I challenged his opinion. "If you're shitting me," I warned him, "I'll kick the shit out of you."

"No shit," he said earnestly.

I considered the idea, then looked at him. "How should I ask her?" I said.

"The important thing," he told me, "is not to seem nervous."

Like myself, Stevens was a virgin in 1976. Our experience of sex was limited to the instruction we had received in Health Class (taught by Mr. Williams, who had transported Stevens, myself, and the other hundred boys enrolled in gym at Ballentine Hill High School out to his farm, on three separate occasions, so that we might observe the correct method of putting a condom on a horse), a package of playing cards (owned by George Furtlong), and a dog-eared paperback book entitled *Man with a Maid* (which Stevens had found in the basement of his house).

Despite this inexperience, I still wanted his advice about asking Bernadette out. Even then, Stevens possessed the ability to give one the impression that he was offering insightful counsel, regardless of what he actually said.

"But what if I am nervous?" I asked him.

"It doesn't matter how you really feel, you have to make it sound like it's no big deal," he told me. "You have to ask her with the same voice you'd ask your mother to pass the catsup."

He then proceeded to instruct me on other matters of which he thought I should be aware: how to dress (t-shirt, jeans, and running shoes – no socks), where we should go (to a movie, but not one in which there was any killing), and finally the correct method of putting my arm around her (not like I was stretching or yawning which is the standard practice of sixteen-year-old boys – but deliberately, as if there was nothing else I would rather do).

"If you know so much about it," I said, "why don't you ask her out?"

"You know I'm not her type," he replied.

We walked away from Bernadette's apartment and I did not have to ask what Stevens meant about not being her type. Stevens was – and still is – visibly overweight. At sixteen, he was perhaps no more than ten pounds too heavy, but in Ballentine Hill this was enough to make him The Fat Kid. Most people called him The Fat Kid when they were describing him, others when they could not remember his name, and some when they were certain he was not near enough to hear. People had been calling him The Fat Kid for so long that he had come to think of himself as The Fat Kid, and at sixteen, he was simply unable to imagine that a girl could be interested in him. We were still talking about Bernadette by the time we arrived at our street. Once there, however, we stopped, because Mrs. Johnson was waving to us.

Mrs. Johnson was a friendly older woman, and for the first ten years of my life I had referred to her as Aunt Barb. Her husband had died of cancer when he was quite young, and she lived alone in the large house next to mine. She kept a beautiful rose garden in front of her house that she watched over protectively. Mrs. Johnson was also an inveterate bubble gum chewer, and in our adolescent eyes, this put her in a class all her own.

"I have something for the two of you," she said as we walked toward her. Mrs. Johnson reached into the pocket of her green gardening pants and produced, to our amazement, Fleer Funny #34.

Times have changed, but in 1976 Dubble Bubble was the only gum worth chewing. Not only did it produce superior bubbles, but each piece of gum came with a comic. These comics were called Fleer Funnies, and Stevens and I had started collecting them when we were both still in grade school. With the conspicuous exception of Fleer Funny #34, we had a complete set of them. I had mentioned this fact several times to Mrs.

Johnson, who chewed almost as much gum as Stevens and I combined.

"I found it this morning," she told us. "Just after breakfast."

After thanking her profusely, we went across the street and sat on Stevens' front porch to discuss the meaning of the comic. As is the case with most of the Fleer Funnies, the meaning of Fleer Funny #34 is almost impossible to determine.

It consists of three frames. In the first frame, a bench is being painted. In the second frame Pud (the ill-starred protagonist of every Fleer Funny) sits down on the bench and begins reading a newspaper. In the final frame, Pud is gone, but his pants remain stuck to the bench. The man who painted the bench has returned, and is looking at Pud's abandoned pants.

"What do you think it means?" Stevens asked me.

"It's about how lazy Pud is," I said. "He sits down on the wet paint, and his pants stick to the bench. Instead of trying to unstick his pants, he leaves them behind."

Stevens shook his head. As was usually the case when we were discussing Fleer Funnies, he produced an unreasonably elaborate interpretation of the comic.

"There is something evil about the painter," he said. "He's painted the bench with some super-sticky paint in order to trap unsuspecting newspaper readers like Pud. The third frame shows the painter returning to capture his prey, but Pud has left his pants behind and foiled the plans of the evil painter."

"I better go," I said. "It's almost time for dinner."

"You should call Bernadette tonight," he said.

"Don't worry."

"She'll say yes," he called after me, as I walked across the street.

That night, after dinner, I prepared to call Bernadette with the same thoroughness that has made me something of a legend at Revenue Canada. I memorized her phone number, wrote a brief outline of what I planned to say, and practised introducing myself several times (to ensure my voice would not crack). I then went downstairs and practised dialing her number without actually touching the dial on the phone. After pouring myself a glass of apple juice (in case my mouth became dry during our conversation), I made the call. I dialed the number quickly, with my eyes almost completely closed, so that I would be speaking to Bernadette before I had a chance to reconsider what I was doing. The phone rang a single time at Bernadette's house, and my mother walked into the kitchen.

"Who are you calling?" she asked. I had already hung up the phone. "No one," I said. "I'm just thinking of calling someone."

"You can do it," she told me. "Boys have been asking girls out since the beginning of time. You will too – there are Certain Things a mother knows."

She kissed me and left the kitchen. However, I did not attempt to call Bernadette again. The anti-climax caused by my mother's untimely entrance robbed me of the courage I'd so methodically worked up, and I went upstairs to my bedroom. Since then, I have given considerable thought to the question of Certain Things. Do such things exist? Buddha Stevens has built a career on the premise that they do. Indeed, the entire Melvin Henderson Incident implies the existence of Certain Things.

Of course, most readers will already be familiar with the Melvin Henderson Incident, which first brought Stevens international notoriety. It happened three years after the events which I am describing, and by that time I had stopped associating with Stevens entirely. We still lived across the street from one another, but almost never spoke. Nevertheless, we continued to attend the same high school (there being only a single high school in Ballentine Hill), and I was there, in the school cafeteria, when the frequently mythologized Melvin Henderson Incident actually occurred.

Mrs. Henderson (Melvin's mother) had collapsed in the bathtub the night before, and had been rushed to the hospital. During the night she had slipped into a coma, and the doctors were not optimistic. Melvin had come to school that day, and brought with him a small green scarf belonging to his mother. Without speaking, he placed it on the table where Stevens was eating lunch. I was sitting at the other end of the cafeteria that day, and although I had already publicly disassociated myself from Stevens, I could not help watching him. The cafeteria became suddenly quiet as everyone stopped chewing. I could feel the eyes of the school on him.

Before that afternoon, a sizable percentage of the student population knew something about the enigmatic talent of Buddha Stevens. They knew he was almost unbeatable at euchre and that he was never wrong about who would win the Stanley Cup. Some had witnessed his ability to predict which questions would be on math tests. However, when Melvin Henderson asked the question that day about his mother, no one knew quite what to expect.

It is usually the practice in biographical writing for an author to identify a "turning point" in the life of his subject – the point at which a person becomes inevitably doomed, or is assured of becoming an unqualified success. Of course, such "turning points" do not really exist. They are fictions created by the biographer in order to foster the impression that the life of his subject has followed a linear progression. I will admit there are certain moments in every life that seem particularly pregnant with the future, but it is only in retrospect that such "turning points" emerge. Quite often, the moments to which people attach the greatest importance in retrospect appear relatively trivial when they are actually occurring. "Turning points" only exist in the past. Unlike people, all moments are created equal.

However, if I were asked to identify a "turning point" in the life of Buddha Stevens, I would most certainly point to that afternoon in the cafeteria of Ballentine Hill High School. It was the pivotal moment of his life. If he had said the wrong thing, Stevens would have remained in obscurity. He would have quietly taken over the operation of his father's hardware store and never left Ballentine Hill. Perhaps eventually, he would have married Doreen Crane, a slightly overweight, but not unattractive girl in our grade. He would never have been interviewed on national television, or owned a house in Forest Hill, or had his picture on the front page of the *Toronto Star* shaking the hand of Jack Nicholson. He would've been exactly like everyone else.

"What is your question?" Stevens asked Melvin that day in the cafeteria.

"It's about my mother."

Stevens closed his eyes and touched the scarf with his fingertips. He moved very quickly, and then was completely still for what seemed like a long time. The cafeteria was utterly silent. Then he looked at me. I have thought a considerable amount about that look. For a long time I wanted to believe it was an apology.

"Mrs. Henderson will live," he said calmly, but loud enough for everyone in the cafeteria to hear him.

Less than a second after Stevens had finished speaking, the principal came on the P.A. and called Melvin Henderson up to the office. Melvin picked up the scarf and walked out of the cafeteria. The only sound was the rubber bottom of Melvin's sneakers moving across the polished floor, but everyone continued to look at Stevens, who had returned to eating his sandwich. No one spoke until Melvin Henderson ran back into the cafeteria less than a minute later and announced that his mother would live. She had been discharged from the hospital with nothing more serious than a warning from her doctor never to eat kiwi fruit again. A huge cheer went up, and the legend of Buddha Stevens was born.

Various stories began to circulate about him. Dorothy Kendall claimed he had known the name of her second cousin's boyfriend without ever meeting him. Mr. Cobb (the shop teacher) revealed that he had been consulting Stevens about lottery numbers for a considerable amount of time. Bob Watson, a notorious storyteller in the tenth grade, claimed to have seen Stevens levitate. It was also at that time that people began to call him Buddha Stevens.

I should perhaps mention it was George Furtlong who first used the name Buddha Stevens. He was describing the Melvin Henderson Incident to some grade nine girls who had not witnessed it, and the name spontaneously occurred to him. Like most people in Ballentine Hill, George Furtlong knew absolutely nothing about Buddhism. He used the name because he had recently seen a picture of the Buddha in the *Encyclopedia Britannica*. George made the connection (as he explained eventually to a reporter from *A Current Affair*) mostly because the Buddha appeared to be overweight (like Stevens), and seemed to have a connection with the supernatural (as did all things Eastern to the provincial gaze of George Furtlong). The name stuck because it combined a mysterious sound with a representational naturalism. It appealed greatly to our literal-minded, northern Ontario town.

It was only a matter of time before the television crews began to arrive. Having been informed of the circumstances under which my friendship with Stevens dissolved, several interviewers asked me to comment, but I declined. Until now, I have steadfastly refused to associate myself with the cult of Buddha Stevens, a cult which was still very much in its infancy when I was attempting to muster the courage to ask Bernadette Mac-Lean out.

"It's Wednesday," Stevens said, after I had told him about my mother's inconvenient entrance into the kitchen and my subsequent loss of nerve. "If you're going to ask her out for this weekend, you better do it soon."

We were standing outside Bernadette's apartment building and I was looking into her window. "I would ask her," I said, "but she might say no."

"Believe me," he said. "She will say yes."

We began to walk home. I reached into my back pocket and look out a piece of Dubble Bubble. I put the gum into my mouth and looked at the comic.

"Let me see it," he said, and I handed it to him.

It was Fleer Funny #30, one of the most common and perplexing of all the Dubble Bubble comics, a comic Stevens and I had discussed on many previous occasions. Indeed, in 1976 it would have been difficult to find a teenager in northern Ontario who had not wondered, at least once, about the meaning of Fleer Funny #30.

In the first frame, Pud is pictured on a roller coaster, sitting behind a woman with blond hair. In the second frame, the roller coaster is in mid-descent, but the woman's hair has somehow transferred itself to Pud's head. It was the moving hair that Stevens and I always disagreed about. The explanation I proposed for the cartoon was simple: the woman was so scared that her hair had jumped off her head. The author of the comic had taken a phrase that is usually meant figuratively ("it scared the hair right off me") and represented it literally.

Stevens disagreed. He concocted a needlessly elaborate scenario to explain the moving hair. According to Stevens, the woman on the roller coaster had been undergoing treatment for cancer, which caused her hair to fall out completely. PUD takes her to the fair in an effort to cheer her up. However, his good intentions end in disaster, when the woman's wig suddenly falls off during the middle of the ride.

In short: I preferred a reasonable explanation while Stevens advocated a fantastic theory. It is this absolute disregard for rationality which distinguished him, even at an early age. Doubtless, Stevens' readings of Fleer Funnies may seem like an inconsequential detail to many readers. But it is such detail that most tellingly displays one's character. Anyone can act intelligently in a context that obviously calls for intelligence, or be heroic in a situation that demands a hero – but only a truly intelligent person displays intelligence in the smallest things. I offer my observation of Stevens' reading of Fleer Funnies not as evidence but as detail: as an illustration of the difference between a man like myself, and one who will claim, on national television, that he knows the future. It should be plain that a person could not even consider the career that Stevens has successfully undertaken without possessing a very real capacity for indiscretion, and more than a casual disregard for everything that is reasonable.

However, when I handed Stevens Fleer Funny #30 that day, this time he did not debate the meaning of it with me. He looked at it, and his eyes became very far away. It was like he had fallen asleep standing up, with his eyes wide open. After a moment, he seemed to jerk himself awake. He looked at me, and it was then that I realized he had become suddenly, terribly afraid.

"You look like shit," I told him. "Are you all right?"

"I'm fine," he replied, and then after a moment, "My stomach hurts."

I tried to engage him in a discussion of Fleer Funny #30, but he seemed uninterested. He still held the comic in his hands and was staring at it, like he was seeing it for the first time.

"So," I said, after a while. "You really think I've got a chance with Bernadette?"

The question seemed to surprise him. He looked at me, and it seemed as though he was about to say something but changed his mind. "Sure," he said finally. "You should call her tonight."

We hardly spoke for the rest of the walk home. We reached our houses and I noticed Mrs. Johnson was not outside taking care of her roses. I said goodbye to Stevens and walked up my driveway. My parents were not at home. There was a note on the kitchen table from my mother saying that she and my father had gone shopping. I finished reading the note and realized the perfect opportunity for calling Bernadette had just presented itself. With only a minimal amount of preparation, I made a second attempt to call her. Again, the phone at her house rang a single time before I had to hang up.

Someone was ringing my doorbell. I went to the door. I thought that perhaps it was Stevens, coming over to give me some last-minute advice about what to say to Bernadette.

But it was not Stevens.

It was Mrs. Johnson.

She told me my parents had been in a car accident. My father was dead and my mother was seriously injured. Mrs. Johnson said she had come to take me to the hospital to see my mother.

I pushed past her and ran across the street. Stevens was sitting on his front porch, like he was waiting for me.

"Why didn't you tell me?" I asked him.

He looked away.

"You should have said something," I told him. "If you knew, you should have said something."

He shook his head and stood up to go inside. But before he could open the door, I grabbed him by the hair and dragged him down the front steps to the driveway. I do not recall where I hit him first, but soon he was on the ground and I was kicking him.

"Please stop," he managed to say.

"You shithead," I yelled, and kicked him harder.

Mrs. Johnson came running from across the street and eventually dragged me away. She pulled me into her house and then called an ambulance. Stevens was in the hospital for two weeks. I did not visit him, despite the fact that my mother was on the same floor at the hospital and I had to walk past his room every day. I overheard people talking about his injuries, but I did not listen very carefully. I gather they were somewhat serious.

I am not proud of the fact that I once almost killed Buddha Stevens. I am not a violent man, and I have asked myself many times what caused me to behave in such a reprehensible manner. I suppose the best – the only – explanation I can provide is that I was under extreme emotional duress and lost control of myself. I needed someone to blame, and Stevens happened to be a convenient outlet for my anger. Of course, I was not actually hitting him, but rather, the unacceptable fact that my father was dead.

I suppose many readers will regard this merely as a confession. It is certainly an admission of guilt, but I do not require absolution. I write what I write in an attempt to diminish, at least in some measure, the mystique in which Stevens has carefully cloaked himself. If his legend continues to grow at the rate it has for the past ten years, there is no telling what heights he will attain. He already seems well on his way to becoming the Edgar Cayce of the twenty-first century. Like myself, Buddha Stevens will be thirty-four this year. He is only beginning.

However, I do not wish to add my voice to the many who have already convincingly shown that Buddha Stevens' predictions lack substance. Stevens' reply to such critics is always the same: they have not interpreted his prophecies correctly. It is an ingenious and perfect defence for a soothsayer. Buddha Stevens has learned the lesson of the Fleer Funnies well. His replies never mean a single thing, and the possibility of misinterpretation is always present. As most readers are probably aware, I recently attended one of his "lectures" and saw him perform. Although I would not call it an enjoyable experience, I was actually quite impressed. Stevens would perhaps challenge my use of the word "performance" in connection with his practice, but there was something decidedly theatrical about it.

He was speaking at Convocation Hall at the University of Toronto, and although it is a large auditorium, tickets for the evening sold out within ten minutes of going on sale. I suppose Stevens would claim it was more than a coincidence that I got through to the box office with only a single phone call. It was actually a spur of the moment decision on my part. I was looking through the morning paper while eating breakfast, and I happened to see an advertisement for Buddha Stevens. I had no idea that he was going to be Toronto, or when the tickets went on sale. Just before I left for the office I called the number listed in the paper and purchased a single ticket. It was not a decision to which I devoted a great deal of thought. I dialed the number quickly, barely even looking at the telephone.

The lecture began at eight o'clock and I arrived, as is my usual practice, fifteen minutes early. I must confess I have never seen Convocation Hall surrounded by such a carnivalesque atmosphere. There were hot dog vendors, street musicians, an amateur fortune teller (The Magnificent Mangepanne), T-shirt salesmen (the shirts were green, and on the front of them there was a drawing of a svelte Stevens sitting cross-legged), a yellow school bus (a large contingent of senior citizens from Plattsburg, Ontario, were disembarking slowly), several homeless people asking for spare change, booksellers (selling *Seeing Is Believing*, Stevens' book containing his predictions for the twenty-first century), and a very tall man riding a unicycle while he juggled bowling pins.

I made my way through the crowd and into the building. An attendant – wearing an impressively long black robe with the words "Buddha Stevens" printed on the front of it in quite elegant, fluorescent yellow letters – directed me to my seat.

"No photographs," he warned me. "Or you're out."

I had an aisle seat, near the back of the hall and to the left of the stage. At the end of each aisle, very near the stage itself, there were a number of microphones that had been strategically placed so the audience could ask Stevens questions. The crowd was still making its way inside when the lights suddenly went down. It became very quiet in the darkness, and a spotlight suddenly switched on. It was trained on Buddha Stevens himself, sitting cross-legged in the middle of the stage, with his eyes downcast, in that characteristic posture that never ceases to remind me of a certain photograph in the *Encyclopedia Britannica*.

He had not changed much. He was older, perhaps heavier, and his curly hair was considerably more successfully managed than it had been in high school. During the show, he moved confidently across the stage speaking into a black wireless microphone, and looking directly into the eyes of his audience. He will never be a graceful man, but Stevens has managed to cultivate a rather compelling stage presence. It is not an effect produced by a single gesture, but by a certain assurance of movement; an excessive calm.

I cannot recall everything he said. He began with a series of vague pronouncements about the environment, and then made some general statements concerning the future of Quebec. He also implied that the Montreal Canadiens would not win the Stanley Cup ("unless the river comes around again"), and that the string of Blue Jays World Series victories might have come to an end ("unless the tree changes its leaves"). As always, he did not state anything explicitly.

I do not recall exactly when I stood up and made my way down the aisle toward a microphone.

While I waited for my turn, Stevens continued to answer several questions that required him to move around the theatre. He touched the hand of a young woman ("Am I pregnant?"), the baseball cap of a missing child ("Is he still alive?"), a woman's left breast ("Is it malignant?"), an earring that belonged to a dead grandmother ("Is she with Jesus?"), and made some vague statements about a younger man's lack of success in business.

"I have a single question," I said into the microphone when it was my turn to speak. "A simple question."

Stevens was at the other side of the stage, and I think he must have recognized my voice. He turned around slowly, and looked at me for what seemed like a long time before speaking.

"What do you want to know?" he asked.

"I want to know about Certain Things," I replied. "I want to know if there are Certain Things in the universe."

I am not sure what I expected him to say. It was, I know, foolish for me to think he would debate an abstruse metaphysical topic right there, in front of hundreds of his most loyal followers. I suppose I thought he would give me either a straightforwardly flippant reply, or avoid the question entirely, and that either of these would make him look foolish. However, he gave neither a glib nor an ambiguous answer. He did something I never would have guessed.

He smiled.

"I know why you're asking that question," he told me. "It has nothing to do with the future. It's about the past."

I suppose I must have nodded because people in the audience began to whisper to each other. I was rapidly becoming another example of Buddha Stevens' remarkable powers of insight. He walked across the stage and stood next to me.

"What do you think about the Certain Things?" he said, and put his hand out to touch me. It rested heavily on my shoulder.

I leaned forward and began to speak into the microphone, but someone had shut it off.

"Was it not a Certain Thing that you would come to this place tonight and ask me this question?" he said into his wireless microphone. "Was it not a Certain Thing ever since that afternoon when I predicted your father's death and you didn't believe me?"

I could hear the surprised whispers of the audience. I shook Stevens' arm off my shoulder and grabbed his microphone. I removed it easily from his chubby hand, and was beginning to tell the audience the truth about what had happened, when a number of men in black robes took hold of me. They relieved me of the black microphone and dragged me toward the exit. As they carried me out, I could hear Stevens telling his audience about how we grew up together, and about how, even then, people were resentful and afraid of his abilities. I could not make out exactly what he was saying but I recognized the tone of his voice immediately: it was the same voice with which he used to ask his mother to pass the catsup.

The attendants pushed me through the doors of Convocation Hall and left me on the sidewalk, where photographers from all the major Canadian newspapers were waiting. Three days later, the *Toronto Star* article appeared. They had interviewed – of all people – Melvin Henderson, who said that I had always hated Buddha Stevens, and once even tried to kill him. He implied that perhaps I had gone to Convocation Hall that night to make a second attempt.

.Fortunately, my colleagues at Revenue Canada are intelligent enough not to believe everything they read.

I suppose that even I, at one time, believed that Buddha Stevens could know the future. I now see the absurdity of that notion, and the fact that he has used the story of my father's death to fuel his own legend sickens me. It is ridiculous for him to claim there is a disaster brewing each time he feels unwell. I have neither the time nor the inclination to catalogue the numerous occasions when he looked sick as we were walking home, and nothing ruinous occurred. It is also interesting to note that – although Stevens insisted repeatedly that we would – Bernadette MacLean and I never went on a date. After my father's death, I stopped walking past her apartment and never again looked up at her window. I made sure I always went home by the short, most direct route.

THE OBITUARY OF PHILOMENA BEVISO

BEVISO, Philomena Rosaria – At her home in Toronto,[1] suddenly,[2] on Thursday, August 19, 1985, in her 78th year. Daughter
of the late Carmella and Paul Luciani[3] and beloved wife of

---

[1] Philomena was making pizza dough when she felt the pain in her left arm. She
dropped the dough and tried to steady herself by gripping the kitchen counter. Then
her knees buckled and she fell to the floor. The pain spread through her chest and she
found she could not stand up. She lay on the floor and looked at the ceiling.

"It's very dirty," she said out loud to the empty kitchen.

Costanzo Beviso was out in the garden and did not know what had happened until
it was too late. He walked into the kitchen carrying a large cucumber and a basket of
green beans. He dropped them both when he saw his wife. He knelt down on the floor
and listened for her breathing before calling the ambulance. Then he went back into
the kitchen and closed Philomena's eyes.

[2] Theodoro Beviso arrived at his parents' house before his mother's body was taken
away by the ambulance. It was her third heart attack and they had been told to expect
it. His father was sitting at the kitchen table and staring at the pizza dough in his hands.

"We knew it was coming," said Theodoro.

"We knew," his father replied, without moving his eyes. "But not today."

[3] It had just stopped raining in the small Italian town of Montescalgosio when Carmella
DiCicco told Paulo Luciani, the carpenter's son, that she was pregnant. Paulo did not
speak for at least a minute and Carmella got ready to run. She was afraid he had gone
crazy and might try to kill her. Like all the women in Montescalgosio, Carmella was
well informed about the disastrous effect the news of childbirth could have on a man.
Just three years earlier, Giovanni Mimesi (her second cousin) went suddenly blind for
two weeks after his wife informed him she was pregnant with his fourteenth child.
Carmella held her breath while Paulo looked up at the sky and did not speak. But Paulo
Luciani had not become crazy. He was thinking that his father had warned him about
such things. Paulo liked Carmella but he was not quite ready to get married. He
wanted to see the rest of the world (or at least Rome, fifty miles to the north) before
settling down. But then Paulo saw himself as a father and smiled at Carmella, who
looked ready to defend herself.

"What do you want to name her?" he asked.

"Philomena," replied Carmella (it was her mother's name). "If it's a girl," she added.

"It'll be a girl," said Paulo.

They were married two weeks later, and although they did not approve of the marriage, Carmella's parents gave the couple a small donkey named Baroni (The Baron) as
a wedding present. The baby came six months after the wedding.

Costanzo.[4] She will be sadly missed by her son Theodore[5] and her grandson Paulo.[6] Former employee of Beviso Shoes[7] and

---

[4] It was raining in Mondorio when Philomena ran into the shoe store (it had no name because it was the only shoe store in the town) and saw Costanzo for the first time. She did not know his name because she was from Montescaligosio (a town ten miles to the west) and had never been to Mondorio before. She had been sent to Mondorio by her mother to get some spices from a woman, and it began to rain as she was walking by the shoe store. Costanzo was the only one in the store that day, and he was working on a very old pair of shoes belonging to a man named Rizzotto, when she ran through the front door. Philomena asked him if she could wait in the store until the rain stopped, and because she had been running with a bowl of spices, she sneezed five times in rapid succession. Costanzo looked at the sneezing girl. He said she could stay in the store forever if she wanted. He was just a boy then, but he already had blue eyes that were like flashlights and Philomena blushed uncontrollably when he looked at her (but she did not make the comparison, because she had not yet seen a flashlight). He put aside his shoes and brought out a covered plate from behind the counter. They sat in the doorway of the shoe store, eating olives and watching the rain. Costanzo asked her to marry him two years later, but Philomena had made up her mind that afternoon.

[5] Theodore was born in the living room of a small house on Beverly Street in Toronto. It was a long labour and Philomena was certain she would die. Costanzo got home from his job at the picture-frame factory during the fourth hour of contractions.

"You did this to me," Philomena screamed when he walked through the front door. "You did this, you *gambastorte*."

Gambastorte is the worst thing that you can call a man in the town of Montescalgosio. It means "crooked legs," and although it can refer to a man's lack of success in business, it usually means he is impotent. Costanzo, however, seemed imperturbable. He sat calmly beside his wife and held her hand for forty-one hours while she called him unimaginable names. Costanzo remembered the stories his mother had told him about his own birth. This was the way all of the babies in his family were born: they were never less than ten pounds.

[6] Paulo was born in a hospital. His mother was a thin, *mange cake* woman named Sandra Leckie whom Theodora had met when he was in high school. Philomena disapproved of their marriage mostly because she did not believe the small girl would be able to bear Theodora's huge children. She was only partly right, having underestimated the advances medical science had made in the thirty years since her labour in the house on Beverly Street. The thirteen-pound baby boy was delivered after only thirty hours of contractions and Sandra survived the Caesarean section.

"My God," she said, when it was all over. "I'm not doing that again."

"Just like a flashlight," Philomena said, when she held her grandson for the first time.

[7] When she and Costanzo got off the boat at Ellis Island in 1929, Philomena already knew she was pregnant with Theodore. They travelled to Toronto, where she had an aunt, and they moved into a small house on Beverly Street with five other families. Costanzo got a job at a picture-frame factory for eight dollars a week and Philomena had the baby. They had only been in Toronto for a year when Costanzo heard there was a shoe store for sale downtown. He took Philomena and the baby to look at it one afternoon.

They spent a long time there that day talking to Augustus Beviso, the man who owned the store. He said he was going back to Italy because his mother was dying, and Costanzo offered to run the store for him while he was gone.

daughter-in-law of the late Augustus Beviso.[8] Resting at the
Cardinal Funeral Home (366 Bathurst at Dundas) 2-5 and 7-9
Monday and Tuesday.[9] Funeral service 3 pm, Wednesday,

Philomena was against the idea. "What about your other job?" she asked him. "What
about the eight dollars a week?"

"But Philomena," he said, turning his blue eyes on her like flashlights (which she
had still not yet seen), "it's shoes, and I'm a shoemaker. It could lead to great things."

The next day they went down to Beviso Shoes and – after several hours of delicate
negotiations (during which Philomena threatened, no less than six times, to walk out
of the store, taking her husband with her) – Costanzo signed a handwritten contract
entitling him to eighty percent of the profit from Beviso Shoes until Augustus Beviso
returned from Italy

For the next ten years they ran the business together. Costanzo told customers he
could restore any pair of shoes, no matter how worn, to their original condition, and
Philomena began importing shoes from Italy not available anywhere else in the city.
Soon Beviso Shoes became the place to go in Toronto for Italian footwear.

But there was no news from Augustus Beviso.

It was during the eleventh year of Augustus Beviso's absence that Costanzo told
Philomena he considered himself to be the owner of Beviso Shoes.

"Be careful," Philomena told him. "You only think you own it."

It was also around that time that Costanzo began to have the nightmares. He never
talked about them, but Philomena knew when he was having one. He would roll onto
his back and say "Beviso" quite clearly before breaking into a cold sweat and waking up.

"You can't keep this up," Philomena said to him finally. "We have to find out what
happened to Augustus Beviso."

Philomena began to make inquiries, both in Italy and in Canada. After she failed to
find anyone named Beviso, she made an appointment with a lawyer. The lawyer told
her that the only way they could own Beviso Shoes was to be a relative of Augustus
Beviso. When he heard this, Costanzo became very depressed and could hardly sleep
at all.

[8] It was Philomena who came up with the plan. The first thing she did was book passage for her family on a boat to Italy, and take all their money out of the bank. They
closed down the shoe store and told people they were going to Italy for a vacation. Two
months later, on their way back to North America, Philomena threw their passports,
birth certificates, and her husband's driver's licence into the ocean. When they landed
at Ellis Island, Costanzo said they had been robbed and the American government
agreed to issue each of them new passports. He said their last name was Beviso, and
the immigration official had to believe him. To the American government, Costanzo
was just another Italian without papers. They returned to Toronto and re-opened the
shoe store. Five years later, Costanzo went down to City Hall and said he was the son
of the late Augustus Beviso. He showed them a long letter in Italian (forged by
Philomena) containing the last will and testament of Augustus Beviso. Costanzo inherited the shoe store.

[9] Two hours after Philomena's body had been driven away in the ambulance, Theodore
received a call from Glen J. Clattenburg, of Cardinal Funeral Homes Ltd. Mr.
Clattenburg expressed his condolences, and reminded Theodore that there were certain practical matters regarding his mother's death that required immediate attention.
Not wanting to disturb his father, Theodoro drove down to meet with Mr. Clattenburg
alone.

August 25, at St. Mary Immaculate Roman Church, 10295 Yonge Street.[10] Internment to follow at Holy Cross Cemetery.

Theodore had heard horror stories about funeral directors, and as a secretary guided him through the expensively decorated funeral home, he prepared himself to be confronted by a slick con man who made his living by preying on the emotionally bereaved relatives of the deceased.

Theodore was surprised to discover that Mr. Clattenburg was a short, slightly fat man who spoke very gently and slowly. He expressed his condolences again and reflected, in passing, on his own mother's death and how difficult such things always were. After agreeing on the wording of the obituary, and the times of the visitation and funeral, Mr. Clattenburg led Theodore into the next room and helped him choose a coffin. It took less than half an hour, and Mr. Clattenburg walked Theodore out to his car.

"There's just one more thing," he said. "You might bring us some better clothes for your mother tonight – we have to start getting her ready."

Theodore drove back to his parents' house. His father had fallen asleep on the couch, and the house seemed very quiet; not at all like the place where he had been a child. He went into his parents' bedroom and opened his mother's closet. All of the dresses looked very similar and he had no idea which one his mother had liked best. It suddenly seemed very important to Theodore for her to be buried in a dress she liked. He sat down on the bed to think, and noticed the digital alarm clock he had bought for his mother as a birthday present eleven years before. The alarm had been set for six-thirty the next morning, the time at which she had been getting up at for as long as he could remember. Theodore switched off the alarm. It was a long time before he felt able to drive back to the funeral home.

[10] Philomena is twenty-seven years old in the black-and-white photograph that was placed on her coffin during the funeral. It was taken on Theodore's third birthday when she realized there was only one other picture of him (taken just after he was born). She took him to the photographer's studio, and because he was offering a two-for-one special that day, she was able to get a portrait of herself for no extra charge. Her long black hair hangs down below her shoulders, and she is wearing a plain white dress. She is looking directly into the camera, and her hands are folded neatly in her lap. Although it looks like she tried to cover it up with some kind of makeup, there is a small love bite visible on her neck, placed there the night before by her husband. She has only been in Canada for four years, and already she has taken over the operation of Beviso Shoes and had a son. She is learning to speak English in the evenings and it will be another twenty-four years until she sees a flashlight.

THE DEAD THING

Jeanne Evans saw the dead thing on a Tuesday evening near the end of January. It was only the second week of the semester but already she was disillusioned. Once again she was teaching "Introduction to Tragedy" and once again it promised to be a frustrating and depressing experience. Each time she taught the course it was the same thing. No matter what she said, students seemed incapable of grasping the meaning of the tragic.

"For Aristotle," she'd told them that night, "tragedy is not about character, but plot."

The students made a note of this.

"A plane crash," she'd told them, "is not a tragedy."

They wrote this down as well.

"Here's what I mean," she went on. "If I walked out of here and was hit by a car, that would be sad – but not a tragedy. At least, not so far as Aristotle was concerned. Now, on the other hand, if I walked out of here on my last day before retirement and got hit by a car, that would be better. If the car was driven by my husband, even better. And best would be if my husband ran me over on my last day of teaching because he was speeding to school in order to pick me up for a surprise party that he'd arranged to celebrate my retirement."

"When did this happen?" said a blond boy near the back of the classroom.

Jeanne looked at the class.

The class was waiting to hear.

Jeanne silently vowed to never teach the tragedy course again.

This year, she knew, she had only herself to blame. In the past she'd not had a choice. The Chairs of English Departments called and she taught what they gave her to teach. Such is the lot of contract faculty. It had been five years since Jeanne had got her doctorate, and although she'd had some good interviews with good schools (or what she'd imagined were good interviews with what she'd told herself were good schools), she'd never got a single offer for a tenure-line job. Which meant that each August she sent out her resumé to the different universities in the area – to Rutgers, to Montclair, to Deane College, to the New School, to NYU, to Princeton, to Temple, once even to Penn – and crossed her fingers that some faculty member would have gone hurtling over the bars of his motorcycle, or skipped town at the last minute, or have been arrested for bank fraud and there would be a course they needed her to teach. But this time she had sent out no applications; this time the idea had been to take the term off to finally turn her dissertation into the book that she knew she needed to publish if she was ever going to get hired.

"The clock is ticking," she'd told David, her husband. "Once you've been disposable you'll stay disposable unless you do something about it. You have to get out early, or not at all."

David nodded and seemed sympathetic but Jeanne could see he was basically through talking about it; he had heard it all before. David worked as a conductor for New Jersey Transit, and tended to approach problems with a simplicity that Jeanne regarded as either wholly effectual or entirely simple-minded.

"Just stay home," he told her, "and write the thing."

It was July, and the two of them were sitting outside in the falling light, in the backyard of the gray shuttered house on Comstock. Jeanne had been staring across the street at the ruins of the old post office, but now she turned to look at David. He was not smiling, Jeanne saw, and she knew he was serious. She told him she might just take him up on his offer. That was exactly the way she put it: "David," she told him, "I might just take you up on your offer."

"Good," he said.

In the distance they could hear the sound of trains.

She looked at him and said, "I hope I can do it, you know. I hope that I have it in me."

"Take the year," he said. "See what happens. A lot can happen in a year."

Without his quite having to say so, Jeanne understood that what they were also talking about was their having a baby.

It had been a sensitive subject between them because there had been a miscarriage. Or, at least, that was what Jeanne believed. But she could not be sure, either about the pregnancy or the miscarriage. She'd been a week late, had taken the test, and got the positive result. This, in her mind, had decided it. Jeanne knew the test would be more accurate if she'd waited longer – if she'd waited two weeks, or even a whole month as the instructions inside recommended – but she had to know. She had been teaching that year at Rutgers, and had gone in that night prepared to lecture, but threw up five minutes before class began. She'd taken her books out and set her notes down on the podium – already she'd taken her wristwatch off and put it to one side so that she could see the time without being seen by the class to have looked – and the nausea had come over her all at once, like a dirty wave. She'd run out of the room and barely made it to the washroom. Eventually one of the girls in the class came in after her and Jeanne called to her through the stall door, saying that the class was cancelled. The bathroom floor was dirty and smelled strongly of urine, but Jeanne felt happy as she knelt there and held back her hair, believing it the beginning of morning sickness. But when she'd stood up to leave, she threw up again. This happened four more times and she had to call David to come and pick her up. It was the flu, and when the fever broke a week later Jeanne knew she'd lost the baby. If there had been a baby at all. She'd told David, shown him the test even, and now she felt stupid, and guilty. It was the thought that she'd taken the test too early that was the worst. Had she tempted fate? The only evidence that any of it had ever happened was the old pregnancy test, with its faded pink line. Eventually Jeanne stopped looking at it but, even afterwards, she carried it around in the bottom of her purse. It seemed to her something picked up in a dream, a remnant of nothing. Still, she did not throw it out until that night when she and David talked about her taking the year off. And just like that, the year had changed. Now it stretched out before her, full of possibility. She thought of Milton then, of the final quatrain of *Paradise Lost*:

> *The world was all before them, where to choose*
> *Their place of rest, and Providence their guide:*
> *They hand in hand with wand'ring steps and slow,*
> *Through Eden took their solitary way.*

She thought of saying so to David, reciting the lines to him, but stopped herself. She would have to explain them, and that would ruin the moment. Still, thought Jeanne, this was how she felt, like she'd been given a second chance. Like she'd been handed a prophecy. So, when August rolled around she did not send out her resumes. Neither did she call the chairs of English Departments in the area to say that she was available to teach anything and everything. She did nothing of the sort. Instead, for the first time in five years, she sat down and began to write, feeling herself lucky. That, somehow, she had managed to avoid the worst, the kind of bad luck that could twist and maim a person.

But then, the week classes began, she'd got a call from the Chair of the English Department at Deane.

"Frankly, I'm in a spot, Jeanne," the Chair told her, not saying hello. The department's Shakespearean had left for South Africa at the last minute and he needed someone quickly.

"Can I call you back?"

"If you're not available, I'll have to find someone else. The class begins today."

"I don't know," she said.

"It's the tragedy course," he told her. "You've done it before."

Jeanne hesitated. Deane was a small, three-year college not far from their house. She'd done what she believed to be patient, good work there, and the Chair liked her. Which meant he offered her the best leftover courses first. To turn him down now – he was clearly desperate – would mean burning bridges. Plus, it was just around the corner. She could walk there in the afternoons, and back in the early evenings. It would not take too much time. It would be a good break.

"All right," she told him, "give me the details."

"Wonderful," said the Chair. "You're saving my life."

After he'd hung up, Jeanne sat for a moment at the kitchen table and then called David, who was at work, shouting over the sound of a train that was somewhere between Edison and Rahway.

"Well," he said, "that's a change of plans."

"They really needed someone," said Jeanne. "And I've taught it before."

"Whatever you think," he shouted, and in the background was the metallic sound of breaks being applied as the train came into the station.

"I know it's a change," shouted Jeanne into the receiver, over the noise, "but I think it's the right thing."

"Jeanne, listen," he shouted back, "I have to go."

"I just don't want to feel like I'm letting you down," she was beginning to say when he hung up.

Jeanne closed her dissertation, which she'd been re-reading, and went upstairs to shower. The class began at three-thirty, and she left the house at two. The class ended at four-thirty, and after it she went to the library. By the time it was five-thirty she was on her way home.

Which is when she saw the dead thing.

It was lying under a leafless tree in front of the old Hungarian Social Club on Somerset Avenue. At first Jeanne thought it was a child, a little thing abandoned to the elements. Like Oedipus, or Moses, or Perdita in Shakespeare's *The Winter's Tale*. It was bigger than a squirrel, but not quite the size of a cat, and fair, nearly blond hair covered the whole of its body. Jeanne had seen it from the other side of the street and had crossed against the traffic with real urgency, imagining a tawdry, desperate scene between teenagers – a messy birth and a desperate abandonment. At the last moment, just as she was about to pick it up and hold it in her arms, she realized it wasn't a baby at all but some animal. It had green slitted eyes and strange hands. It was spread out on its back with its forepaws stretched out over its head, as if it had been reaching up, toward the top of the tree when it died. As if it had known it was soon to die and tried to get to the tree, and had fallen, abjectly, onto its back.

"Poor thing," said Jeanne, half to herself and half to the dead thing. After she'd spoke she waited for a long moment in case the dead thing were not dead at all, to see if maybe the sound of her voice would wake it up, or bring it back to life.

But it didn't, and she went on her way.

David was at home, making dinner. He was standing at the stove and frying pork chops when she came in the door. She kissed him once, on the back of his neck, and he asked how the class went. Instead of answering, Jeanne said again she felt like she was letting him down.

"It's your decision," he told her.

"One course isn't going to kill me," she said. "I can teach it and still write the book. And do whatever else comes up."

"Good," said David.

"If you want me to quit, I'll get on the phone now and say I can't do it."

"I don't mind if you do it."

"I don't think it'll kill me," said Jeanne. "It's just one course."

"I think it's a good idea," said David. "The Chair'll remember it, and when a job comes up, he'll send it your way."

"It doesn't work like that," said Jeanne, and then stopped herself. Now was not the time to give David a lecture on the hierarchies that governed the academic job market. Instead, she told him about the dead thing, about how she had seen it from across the road and had nearly picked it up.

"But it wasn't a baby," she told him. "It wasn't human."

"What was it?"

"Something," she told him.

"You make it sound like an alien."

"This is New Jersey."

David laughed.

They were back to their old selves, thought Jeanne. She had met David six years before, around the time she was finishing her degree. At the time, Jeanne was living in Manhattan, sharing a small one-bedroom with another girl on the upper west side. Each morning she would take the train out to Rutgers and teach her classes; each evening she would take the train back to the city. Then, one morning, the conductor had asked her out instead of taking her ticket. That was David. It seemed incredibly forward to Jeanne for him to do this. More than forward: it was primitive. Jeanne had agreed without quite knowing why. She wondered if it was something she should be worried about, and had asked her roommate, Shelia, about it.

"When he was taking your ticket?" said Shelia. "I bet you could sue for that."

Shelia was the sister of a girl Jeanne had known back home in Ohio. She was a performance artist in Soho, and had both of her nipples pierced. As different as they were, the two made wonderful roommates because they were hardly ever in the apartment at the same time. The only time Jeanne saw Shelia was at breakfast, when Jeanne was leaving to teach and Shelia was just coming in.

"I'm not asking if I should sue him," Jeanne said. "I want to know if I should go out with him."

"Yes," said Shelia.

"You're sure?" said Jeanne.

"A conductor," said Shelia, as if by way of explanation, "that's very rare."

"A conductor," repeated Jeanne, and knew she would show up for the date. It seemed to her a word straight out of Thackeray. Jeanne imagined a conductor to be a portly, bald man, sixty-five, wearing a cap and holding a silver pocket watch. He would give sage advice to wayward travelers and apply the emergency brake at the most dramatic instant, but only as a last result. She knew already that David was none of these things. He was in his thirties, with dark eyes. And he was tall. At dinner she learned that his father had been a conductor as well, and that he had walked into the job after high school. David did not seem particularly proud of this, but neither was he embarrassed. He was something out of a Springsteen song, Jeanne told Shelia, only without the longing. It seemed to Jeanne that David had grown up in New Jersey and had never wanted to leave it – that he had never once looked across the Hudson River and thought to himself that things were sweeter on the other side.

"And who's to say?" Jeanne had said to her roommate. "Maybe they aren't."

"What?" her roommate said. "Are you moving to Jersey?"

"New Jersey," Jeanne corrected her. "David says no one from New Jersey calls it just Jersey."

"So," asked her roommate, "when're you seeing him again?"

"You mean if," Jeanne told her.

Shelia shook her head.

"Next Tuesday," Jeanne confessed.

The truth was that it did not hurt David's chances with Jeanne that he reminded her of a Bruce Springsteen song. Most of what Jeanne knew about New Jersey and the people who lived there were things she had heard in songs or movies. Jeanne had been born in Ohio, and had grown up in South Euclid, one of Cleveland's eastern suburbs. After graduating from high school, her parents had sent her to Queen's University in Canada because her mother had been born there. Jeanne had wanted to go to Cleveland State, with Jimmy, her boyfriend, but in the end her parents had prevailed. At Queen's, Jeanne had been a diligent, successful student, and after graduating she'd applied to Rutgers because her undergraduate advisor had gone there. Once she'd earned her doctorate, Jeanne had found it impossible to even contemplate going back home without a job. But nothing had even come up. Not even in Ohio. So she remained in Manhattan, and lived with Shelia, and taught the courses she could find to teach. But then she met David, and all of that changed. She still wanted her permanent position, still wanted to publish a book, but with David all of that diminished in importance somehow. If it happened, it happened – but if not, there would be something else, something around the corner that was just as fine. Jeanne could not quite believe that this was true, could never be quite as sanguine as David, but that mattered less because she was *with* David, whom she often imagined as a raft, to which she had tied herself.

"But it was a weird thing," said Jeanne to David that night after they had finished dinner. "It *was* strange looking."

"It was a cat?"

"It was the size of a cat," she said. "But it *looked* like a baby."

"But it wasn't."

"If it was a baby – I'd have said that."

"Maybe it was a possum," said David.

"I don't know," said Jeanne. "I don't know what they look like."

"Did it have claws?" said David.

"No," she said, but a moment later she added, "No, I'm not sure it had claws, but it had fingers."

"Then it wasn't a possum," said David. "If it had been a possum, you would have noticed the claws right way."

"The fingers were nice," said Jeanne. "Thin, like the fingers of a piano player."

David laughed.

"I'm not saying it could play the piano."

"Just that if it wanted to, it could?"

"Do they even have possums in New Jersey?" said Jeanne.

"Possums," said David. "You tell me somewhere they don't have possums."

"I've never seen one."

"Or it could have been a ferret, or a monkey," said David.

"It wasn't a monkey," said Jeanne. "It was smaller than that – at first I thought it was a baby."

"Where was it?" said David.

Jeanne told him. "On Somerset," she said. "In front of the old Hungarian social club."

"I'll take a look," said David, then, after a moment, he said, "It really might have been a ferret. You can't tell sometimes, you know, with things out in the wild. The thing with ferrets is, they get out, and once they get out into the wild they turn into wild ferrets."

"I didn't look that closely," said Jeanne. "I can't say what it is."

"*Was*, you mean," said David.

Jeanne looked at him.

"It's dead, after all," said David.

"Well, of course it is," said Jeanne, as if it had never been alive.

Jeanne expected her period would come the following day, and when it did not, she tried to not think about it. Two days passed, and then two more. She tried to act normally and to go about her business, to not say anything to David. Three afternoons a week she went to Deane and tried to teach the tragedy course. They had started with *Oedipus Rex* and had moved on to Shakespeare's *King Lear*.

"I don't know why they can't just talk about it," said one of her students, a girl in the front row wearing a yellow sweatshirt with the word DEANE printed on it in massive black letters. "The whole thing seems a mix up."

"But if they'd talked about it," Jeanne had told them. "There'd be no play – everyone would have lived happily ever after."

The class, it seemed, felt there was nothing wrong with this.

"This is tragedy," Jeanne told them. "It's not about responding to things in a healthy way."

"All she's saying," said a second girl, who was also wearing a massive yellow sweatshirt with a massive DEANE printed on it, "is that it's not very realistic."

Jeanne, again, silently vowed to never again teach the tragedy course.

And yet when Jeanne walked home that night, she was not feeling in the least depressed or disillusioned. She felt happy and decided, in spite of herself, that she was pregnant. And perhaps, she thought, she had been pregnant for some time. The week before, when she had thought the dead thing was a baby and had crossed Somerset Avenue with such impetuousness, running to pick the little thing up in her arms, she'd taken it as a sign that she was about to start menstruating. This was the kind of extreme thing she did. When she was on her period, she would find herself listening to NPR and weeping pitilessly over the difficult circumstances the Iowa farmers faced. Or that a new kind of rose had been discovered by a blind nun in Paraguay. Or that Nichole Kidman had been nominated for an Academy Award. Anything at all. She would find herself marching to the front of the line at the grocery store to give an older man exact change. Or screaming at David because he'd put his dark socks into the wash again with her pink top. She would know that it was happening to her, that she was not acting like herself, but could do nothing about it. The dead thing was that kind of thing – a sign that her period was on the way. Now she began to wonder if it were something else: if her crossing the street with such heedlessness was a maternal instinct beginning to assert itself – that, perhaps, her life had already started to change.

She felt suddenly fond of the dead thing, as if it had somehow been a witness to this change in her, and found herself crossing Somerset to look at it. She found it much as she'd left it. There were no signs of decomposition. No flies or ants, and not even a smell. Even its eyes were still intact. Jeanne had only the vaguest idea of how things decomposed – she recalled, distantly, a biology teacher saying something about the enzymes in one's stomach eventually getting out of control – but took it as a good sign that the dead thing appeared to have been untouched by anything, even time. It looked nearly serene under the tree, as if the desperation to reach the tree that Jeanne had detected in it the day before had passed. It still lay on its back, with its arms and fingers stretched out before it, but now it seemed to have somehow accepted its resting place. Jeanne told it goodbye, and resisted the urge to cover it with some of the leaves which had just started to fall, as if it were going to bed for the night.

"So," said David at dinner that night, "I saw your dead thing."

"My dead thing," snorted Jeanne. "Listen," she told him, "I don't want you looking at my dead thing. You want a dead thing, you get your own."

"I'll hand it to you," said David. "It's weird looking."

"Now, take it easy," said Jeanne. "It's one thing for me to say that my dead thing is weird looking, and it's another thing altogether for you to say it."

David looked at her. "You're in a good mood today."

Jeanne nearly told him then that she was pregnant. "What can I say, staying home agrees with me."

"I'm glad to hear that," said David.

"Anyway," said Jeanne, as if to change the subject, "back to the dead thing."

"Right," said David with mock seriousness.

"What is it?" she asked him.

David clasped and unclasped his hands. "I don't know," he said.

Jeanne looked at him.

"But it is dead," he told her.

And then they both laughed.

So it was the dead thing became a kind of joke between them. Jeanne waited for her period, and taught the tragedy course, and each time she walked to school she made a point of walking past the dead thing.

"So," Jeanne would tell him, "I saw the dead thing today."

"And?" David would ask.

"Looking good," Jeanne would say.

"Well," David would say. "Give him my regards."

Or, David would give the report.

"The dead thing's still there," he said. "There were some ants on its feet, but it didn't seem to bother it at all."

"What a good dead thing," Jeanne replied. "So at home with its own decomposition."

"All dead things should be that way," said David.

"But they aren't," said Jeanne.

"Because they haven't been brought up that way."

"Because of the attention," said Jeanne. "It's the attention that makes the difference."

It became a kind of game, but Jeanne also knew that there was more to it, that it was a way of waiting. She felt like she was treading water. They talked about the dead thing as if it hadn't changed, but actually that was not the case. The changes in the dead thing began with its fur, which thinned at first, and then fell off in dirty-looking clumps. Then the vermin had got to it. Soon there was a dark line around the middle of the dead thing's abdomen, and a little tear at its side, where something – a rat, imagined Jeanne, without quite being able to say so out loud – had bitten into it. Rather than seeming repellent, the process captivated her. She was fascinated, the way she had been fasci-nated with the mummies she'd seen at the MET back when she lived in the city. In this respect, Jeanne felt she was like every-one else; she'd gone to the museum on a regular basis – it was a good way, her roommate Shelia had advised her, to meet men – and had noted the mummy was always the most popular exhibit. School children, elderly men and women who got in for free, the singles who cruised the exhibits – none of them could resist the mummy. Jeanne knew this was because the mummy, like the dead thing, was dead. It had crossed over. It was what the journey looked like. Jeanne knew that the dead thing held for both her and David a morbid appeal which expressed itself through the tasteless updates they gave each other about it, or in the games they would play, like the series of children's books they had made up one night which featured the dead thing: *Good Night, Dead Thing*; *Where the Dead Things Are*; *The Runaway Dead Thing*, *The Dead Thing at the End of the Book*; *Pat the Dead Thing*; *The Dead Thing in the Hat*; *The Velveteen Dead Thing*; *Winnie the Dead Thing and the Blustery Day*.

"Any joke," Jeanne had told her tragedy class, "is a tragedy in miniature."

They were now done with *Lear* and moving on to *Macbeth*, and she had been trying to get them to recall the Sophocles play with which she had started the course. The experience of reading it seemed to have become somehow a distant, irrecoverable memory. Still she tried. Thebes was beset by a plague, she reminded the class, and Oedipus resolves to track down the source, no matter where it leads him – and it leads to him.

"That's the punch line," she told them.

The class stared back; no one, Jeanne noted, made note of it.

"It's the kind of joke at the end of which, instead of laughing, you tear out your eyes," she said.

That *was* a joke, but not a single student laughed.

After a month of her period being late, Jeanne decided it was time to give herself the test. David had left early that morning, as usual, and Jeanne was alone in the house. She sat down on the toilet to wait. Five minutes later, she turned the test over and saw the double pink line.

Right away she got on the phone to the doctor.

"I can't take you this week," said the nurse. "You're only four weeks late and we see women at six, when there's a better chance of hearing the heartbeat."

"Could I just come in, to make sure the baby's fine?"

"You can go ahead and assume you're pregnant," the nurse told her, "but the doctor can't tell you anything about the baby yet. He can look at *you* as many times as he pleases, but if there's no heartbeat there's no baby."

Jeanne told her about the pregnancy test.

"Has there been a problem?" said the nurse, in a different tone. "Has there been bleeding?"

"No," said Jeanne, as if she wished there had been.

"Shall I see what we have open next week?" the nurse asked.

Jeanne knew there was nothing else to be done, so she took the appointment. Then, too antsy to do any work, she went for a walk. It was a warm November day and the leaves covered the sidewalk. Before long, she found herself looking at the dead thing.

"I'm going to have a baby," she told it. "I'm pregnant."

The dead thing lay on its back and did not move.

"Maybe," she said, "I'll name it after you." She laughed at that, and then stopped. It was a terrible thing to say, she realized, and as she walked away she resolved to have nothing further to do with the dead thing.

But when David came home that night, he had with him a large book.

"Jeanne," he said. "I've made a discovery." He opened the book. "It's a cuscus," he told her. "The dead thing has a name – look."

Jeanne saw that David had, indeed, found out what the dead thing was. In each of the photographs the dead thing was not dead at all, but shown on a tree branch, or the bottom of a tree, or next to a leaf, but always with its hands out and its head cocked to one side, as if it were listening intently.

David was reading about it. "The cuscus is an unusual pha-langer that is often mistaken for a monkey. It has a rounded head, small ears almost buried in its head, protruding yellow-rimmed eyes, short muzzle and a yellow nose. About the size of a large domestic cat and with a large prehensile tail, it makes good use of its voice. It has been suggested that its name refers to its scolding or 'cussing,' but in fact it was originally couscous, the French rendering of the aboriginal New Guinea name. Although monkey-like, especially in its face, a cuscus shows its relationship to the kangaroos not only in the female having a pouch but also in the hind foot. This is used for grasping branches and is more like a human hand, the long first toe being thumb-like and particularly strong. But the second and third toes are bound together by skin (that is syndactylous) and their claws are used, as in kangaroos, for combing the fur."

"That's it," said Jeanne unsteadily, when he had finished read-ing, "That's the dead thing."

David sat down at the table. "What is it?" he said. "What's the matter?"

Jeanne told him about having taken the pregnancy test. There was a still and a silent moment between them, and then David clapped his hands three times. All that day Jeanne had worried about telling him, that he would make too much of a fuss, or that he would not believe her. That he would tell her to take another test and that he would watch her the whole time to make sure she'd done it right. But he did none of these things.

He clapped three times, and started to laugh.

"Didn't I tell you?" he said. "Didn't I say it would all be fine?"

"Take it easy," said Jeanne, although she was not quite able to stop herself from smiling. "Until we get to the doctor, nothing's for certain."

"Right," said David. "But still…"

"We go Monday," Jeanne said.

"Monday," said David.

"Until then, we take it easy."

"OK," said David.

"That means acting normal," she told him. "Until we hear."

The next day, Jeanne lectured on Macbeth's famous soliloquy.

"When Macbeth says, 'Out, out brief candle,'" she told the class, "you have to think of candles the way they were at the beginning of the seventeenth century – short, thin, twisted, easily extinguished, and not shedding much light."

"That's really depressing," said the girl who'd been wearing the massive yellow Deane sweatshirt.

"All of this stuff is depressing," said the girl beside her.

"That's the whole point," Jeanne said. "If, when you're reading the play you're agonizing with Macbeth, you're reacting correctly – that's catharsis." She printed the word on the blackboard. "Aristotle thought that's what tragedy provided," she told them. "That when you watched a tragedy, when you got emotionally involved with what's going on onstage, it has a purgative effect. That it provided a useful evacuation, a good riddance."

"Like throwing up," said a boy near the back.

"Yes, but up here," said Jeanne, and pointed to her head.

"That *is* disgusting," said the girl at the front.

The class, Jeanne noted, had stopped writing down anything she said. Some had not even bothered to bring their notebooks to class.

Then, it was Monday. Jeanne and David went to the doctor together, and David drove them. This was unnecessary because
the hospital was closer than both Deane College and the train
station – they really should have walked. But driving seemed
the right thing to do. As if there might be a chance of the baby
coming home with them that day or it had become, suddenly,
risky for Jeanne to walk anywhere.

The waiting room was tiny, and rectilinear, filled with gray
and black metallic chairs. Along the far side of the room there
was a wide, white counter where three women sat behind
computers and answered telephones. It was not quite eight-
thirty in the morning and although Jeanne had imagined they
would have the first appointment, there was already another
couple there. The other couple were about the same age as
they were – in their late twenties, or early thirties – and when
Jeanne and David came into the office they both smiled
broadly, as if they'd been sitting there for some time and had
started to find their own company tiresome. David went with
Jeanne up to the desk and watched her tell the receptionist
her name with a kind of taunt awareness that had started to
both frighten and annoy Jeanne. The receptionist gave Jeanne
a form and told them to have a seat. And then, because it
somehow seemed rude not to, they sat down across from the
other couple.

"I'm W.B.," said the man, "and this is Melinda."

"David," said David, and nodded.

"Congratulations," whispered Melinda to Jeanne.

"Thank you," said Jeanne.

"On the baby," added Melinda.

Jeanne nodded in a noncommittal way and began applying
herself to the form. "They need the insurance card," she told
David. "Did you bring it? They need to photocopy it."

David veritably leaped out of his chair and produced it. He began walking over to the counter to hand it to the nurse.

"No, not now," Melinda called after him. "They take it when you give your form in, and it'll all go in with your file. If you bring it up now, they'll just hand it back to you and tell you to hold onto it until you hand in your form."

David looked at Jeanne as if to ask whether Melinda were a reliable source.

Jeanne shrugged.

David sat back down, somehow deflated.

Jeanne turned back to the form, and as she did she saw W.B. wink at David. It was the kind of wink that acknowledged that women, all women, were a wild, entropic force in the universe at all times, and more so when they were pregnant.

"Have you got babyhead?" asked Melinda. "I've got babyhead – I can't keep my mind on anything."

"No," Jeanne told her. "I'm fine."

"Give it time," said W.B., winking.

David smiled back.

"This one," said W.B., referring to Melinda, "when we were having our first, put diesel in our Highlander. That was the end of that."

Then both Melinda and W.B. laughed; it was, plainly, a story they'd told before.

David laughed also.

"So, how many do you have?" said David.

W.B. held up two fingers.

"Your first?" said Melinda.

David nodded and looked at Jeanne, who had resolved to pretend the other couple did not exist.

"I knew it," said Melinda. "Didn't I say it, when they came in? I said, here's a couple of rookies."

"Is it that obvious?" said David.

Both Melinda and W.B. laughed again.

"What do you do?" W.B. asked David.

While David was telling him, Melinda leaned forward and told Jeanne: "Get used to the babyhead. And be ready for anything. When I had my first, something happened to my spine when it was coming out and I couldn't move my arms for a year."

"That's horrible," said Jeanne.

"It happened right out of the blue," Melinda told her. "One minute I was having the baby, and the next I was paralyzed from the neck down."

"You were paralyzed?" said Jeanne.

"It was mainly my arms," said Melinda. "It happens to a small percentage of all women."

"Let me tell you," said W.B., in a confidential tone that made it plain he was referring to the difficulties the couple had encountered while trying to have sex again, "it was no picnic."

Jeanne was reapplying herself to the form. "Date of LMP," she muttered, to herself.

"Last menstrual period," said Melinda.

"I know what it is," Jeanne told her.

Melinda seemed about to say something.

"So," said W.B., "what're you having?"

"Actually," Jeanne said, looking up, "we don't even know if we're having it yet."

It took a moment, but then Melinda was standing and crossing over to the other side of the waiting room, as if she were intent on getting away from Jeanne. But then, just as she was about to sit down, she stood back up again and headed back, asking Jeanne if she'd really thought about what she was doing.

"I'm trying to fill out a form," said Jeanne.

"Leave it alone," said W.B..

"If she's not going to think this through," said Melinda, "I'm going to make her."

Out of one of the white doors came a nurse who called out Melinda's name. She allowed W. B. to turn her around and, in a hangdog kind of way, to be led in to see the doctor.

"I know you're nervous," said David to Jeanne when they were gone, "but you don't have to make it sound like you're having an abortion."

"What're you talking about?"

"We don't even know if we're having it yet?"

"Well, we don't."

"You don't have to say it."

"Why not? It's true."

"Whether or not its true, you don't have to say it – you make it sound like we're here to get rid of it."

"So what if we were?" said Jeanne. "What gives her the right – it's my body, it's my choice."

"Well," said David, "I want this baby."

"Do you?" said Jeanne. "It doesn't sound like it to me."

Before David could reply, a different nurse appeared and called Jeanne in.

The appointment itself was brief. Jeanne's weight, blood pressure, pulse, and urine were taken. During it all, David sat in a chair in the examination room which seemed to have been put there specifically for husbands to sit in while they waited for their wives' vital signs to be taken. When Jeanne came out of the washroom she had on a kind of hospital gown, a flimsy, antiseptic thing that was tied up at the top and open at the back. The nurse turned to leave and said doctor would be right in. Then she closed the door.

Jeanne sat on the examination table, her legs dangling over the edge.

"How're you feeling?" said David.

"Will you stop asking me that," said Jeanne.

There was a sharp knock at the door and the doctor came in. He shook David's hand, and then asked Jeanne the same questions the nurse had asked: there had been no bleeding, Jeanne told him, no morning sickness, no nothing. She was a month late and she had taken a pregnancy test. The test had been positive.

"Now," said the doctor, "we're going to try to hear the heartbeat. But we might not – and if we don't, it isn't anything to worry about." He smeared some blue jelly on the lower part of Jeanne's belly and turned on a squat-looking machine that sat atop a cart with wheels. The room was filled with a kind of gurgling static and the doctor moved a black wand back and forth across Jeanne's belly. The doctor seemed suddenly to be concentrating intensely, which Jeanne found unnerving. She held out her hand to David, who got out of his designated chair to take it. All of a sudden, as if from a great distance, there was the dull sound of something that sounded like a heartbeat.

"That's it?" said David. "I can hear it."

"Yes," said Jeanne.

They both looked at the doctor.

"That was Jeanne's heartbeat," he told them. "The baby is a tiny, tiny thing – it's got a quick little heartbeat, like a bird."

The doctor shut off the machine. Jeanne felt like she might scream, just to break the silence in the room.

"I'm going to need to see you on Monday," the doctor said a moment later.

"Is there a problem?" said Jeanne.

"No," he told her. "It's nothing to worry about, at this stage.".

"When does it become a problem?" said David.

"See you in a week," the doctor said decisively, as if he were declining further comment.

Jeanne got dressed and they walked down to the parking garage.

"That's bad news," Jeanne told David, when they were in the car.

"You don't know that," said David. "If there had been something to worry about, he would have told us."

"Do you actually believe that?" she asked him.

"He said before he tried to find it that if he didn't hear it, it was no big deal."

"Just because you can't imagine anything bad happening to you," she told him, "doesn't mean it's not going to happen."

They drove home in silence.

That night, after dinner, David gave Jeanne a present.

"I thought we could read it together," he told her.

It was a copy of *What To Expect When You're Expecting*. Jeanne let the wrapping paper fall to the floor and said nothing for a long while as she contemplated the cover, which showed a complacent-looking woman reclined in a rocking chair. A single hand rested atop her perfect belly, and a pillow was wedged into the small of her back. On the wall of the room in which she was sitting were teddy bears. It was a moment of pure expectation, thought Jeanne, a moment devoid of worry and insecurity and everything else except the pure cowlike joy of having a baby. She looked up at David, who was smiling at her in an expectant, nervous sort of way, and tried to smile back. When she found she could not, she looked back at the book and tried to imagine the occasion that the artist had been thinking of when painting his portrait; it seemed to Jeanne that the woman on the cover of the book, with her teddy-beared walls, with the edge of the crib visible in the corner, apparently, had come in and sat down in her baby's nursery, which the couple, apparently, had prepared, had finished preparing, before the woman was anywhere near her delivery date. This was the kind of couple, she imagined, who would have assembled the crib before the baby was even conceived. Such a woman, thought Jeanne bitterly, would never have had to worry about whether a fetus had a heartbeat. For a shrill moment Jeanne wondered if the book might be an accusation, and that the woman on the front cover provided a measure of her inadequacy, that David was telling her to measure up.

"Pride," said Jeanne to her Deane College students, "goes before a fall – we'd all do well to keep that in mind."

They stared back at her.

The following Monday, when it was time to go to the doctor's again, Jeanne and David walked. They went down Comstock to Somerset, and passed the dead thing on their way. They were on the other side of the street, and neither of them said anything about it. Jeanne did not even look. They were onto other things. As they walked, Jeanne told David that she felt like she was going to get her driver's license again.

"At the end of it," she told him, "you get a picture. Think about it – when you go for your license they sign your papers and they take your picture. Nowadays they take the picture right there and hand it to you. Once you have that picture you're safe – you know you're a driver. Same thing with the baby.

"Once you see it in the picture," said David, "you're home free."

"There's nothing to worry about, is there?" said Jeanne.

"I'm not worried," said David.

Jeanne saw it was true. David did not look worried in the least; Jeanne tried to imagine what it felt like to be inside her husband's head. She imagined it an uncomplicated, flat place; that David was unworried because in his head the baby would be there, heartbeat and all, just the way that Edison came before

Rahway when you were on your way into the city and the other way around when you were on your way out.

"I'm sorry to have been such a bitch this last week," she told him.

"Wasn't your fault," he said.

"That other time," said Jeanne. "I probably wasn't pregnant at all."

"What did the doctor say?" said David. "Did you tell him?"

"Sure, I told him, and he said as far as he could tell everything was normal. It was like nothing had happened. That was a good sign, he said."

"Well," said David, "there you have it."

This time the appointment was just as brief. After sitting for a few minutes in the waiting room, the nurse called them in. She took Jeanne's vital signs and a urine sample, and a few minutes later the doctor came into the examination room. Again he shook David's hand and again he asked Jeanne the same questions that the nurse had asked. No, Jeanne said again, no bleeding, no morning sickness, no period.

Then the doctor wheeled over the squat machine, and once again the room was filled with the sound of amplified, gurgling static.

"Just relax," he told Jeanne.

Jeanne tried.

The doctor shut the machine off.

"This is bad," said Jeanne.

"Take it easy," said David.

"I'm afraid that it is," said the doctor in an even voice. "If there's no heartbeat there's no baby."

"Then what is it?" said David.

"I don't think your wife is any danger, but I also don't think the baby is going to come to term."

Jeanne had begun to rock back and forth on the examination table. David went over and held her, his arms around her as if he were holding her together, as if, had he not been standing there Jeanne's body might splinter and fall apart.

"But what about the test?" David said.

"The test is right – Jeanne is pregnant in a manner of speaking, but the baby died, or was never alive to begin with. We have to do a D&C – and then you can try again."

"A dead thing," said Jeanne. "A little dead thing."

"Don't think of it that way," said the doctor. "It was never anything to begin with."

"Maybe we can come back next week?" said David. "Maybe then it'll be there."

"I'm very sorry," he said.

"How can you be so sure?" said David. "What does that thing know at all?"

"Good night, dead thing," Jeanne was saying. "Pat the dead thing."

"We can't leave it in any longer – otherwise you might really never have children," said the doctor to David, then he began to speak very slowly. "You must be careful with her now, I'm going to send in a nurse – and she's going to make sure that you have someone to talk to if you need to talk to someone."

"Where the dead things are," said Jeanne.

The doctor took one last look at Jeanne and then left the room.

Despite his best efforts, David could not keep Jeanne in the office. Once the doctor shut the door behind him, she seemed to come to her senses. She seemed to accept it. She seemed fine. She stopped crying and rocking, and got her clothes on. A nurse came in and said that someone would be right with her, but Jeanne said she was fine, thank you very much, as if she were being offered a sandwich rather than a psychologist. The nurse tried to stop her, or at least slow Jeanne down by reminding her that she had to schedule the D&C. But Jeanne had brushed her off, saying that she would take care of it later. She would call in when she had her appointment book in front of her. David said why not do it now, while she was here, but Jeanne was on her way out of the office. David followed close behind her, and was still right behind her when Jeanne crossed the road against the traffic to the other side of Somerset.

By then she was running, and David was running too,

The dead thing had been moved. Kids. Or drunken college students. Frat boys from Deane College on their way home from the bars. Someone trying to be funny. Someone had bent the dead thing at the waist, and sat it up. Its forepaws were still stretched out over its head, but now, because it was sitting, it looked less like it was diving at the tree than that it had died while in the midst of doing a wave at a baseball game. This impression had been heightened by the fact that whoever had moved the thing had also put on the dead thing's head a tiny Yankee cap. The dead thing's dead eyes were still half open, and its dark irisless eyes looked out on Somerset Avenue as if the street were not a street at all but Derek Jeter or Babe Ruth coming up to the plate.

Jeanne stood and looked at it for a long moment.

"Kids," said David. "Idiots."

Jeanne knew the only thing to be done was to tear out her own eyes, or to rip out her tongue with her own hands. Throw herself off the cliff, like blind Gloucester in *Lear*.

"Come on, Jeanne," he said. "Forget about it."

Jeanne did not move. "Whoever did that," she told David, "they would've had to pick it up. They would have had to bend it in half. It would have been stiff. They *wanted* to do it."

Jeanne knelt down then, and picked the dead thing up herself. She took it into her arms, the way she'd wanted to from the beginning. David tried to stop her, saying something about her not touching it, but then he stopped and followed her home. The two of them like a funeral procession. It was a bright November day and the ground was still soft enough. Jeanne told David where to dig, and in the end the hole was not quite three feet wide, but it was big enough. Jeanne dropped her bundle and nodded once to David. He began filling it in. Somehow, he had come to understand that he, like anyone with a bit part, had no choice in the matter. Something was taking its course. Jeanne watched him fill in the hole, and felt that something massive and indefinable had gone out of their lives.

She did not try to get pregnant after that. For both of them, the pattern of their lives had formed around a single moment in an afternoon. Jeanne knew this happened rarely, if ever. It was something she told her students. Such clarity, writes Aristotle, is the province of literature alone. Even after he'd left her, David would feel sorry for her, but he would always say it was her foolishness that had maimed them and the marriage, *her* fault for stopping that day and thinking the dead thing was a baby. In the settlement, Jeanne won the house on Comstock that David had inherited from his grandmother.

During the day, she taught composition or Introduction to Tragedy, or whatever they had for her at Deane where the Chair was good to her, and at night she would sit alone in the kitchen and look out on the backyard, imagining dark forms outside, moving slowly. Something had changed. She was unable to regret anything.

MY GRANDFATHER'S BEAUTIFUL HAIR

"It's a small animal that eats the hair," my grandfather is saying to me at the kitchen table. "You can't see it, but it's there. It eats the root of the hair."

"It eats the hair?" I ask.

"That's what they say," he tells me.

"Well then," I ask, "where does the animal come from? How do people get infected by it?"

My grandfather looks confused, then angry; as if I am asking a question to which I should already know the answer. "It comes from combs – dirty combs you find on the street," he says.

I can tell that he is not completely certain about how the creature gets onto people's heads. He explains that he cannot remember all of the details concerning the animal. He read about it last week in the *Toronto Star*. He says that he thinks the animal attaches itself to discarded combs because these seem like a logical habitat for an animal that lives on hair. He agrees – when I question him further – that the weak part of this hypothesis is that it requires a great number of people to brush their hair with combs they find on the street.

"I'll find the article," he says to me, getting up from the kitchen table and walking into the laundry room where my grandparents keep the old newspapers. "You'll see."

"We're about to eat," my grandmother says to him. "Find it later."

My grandfather does not reply. He pretends not to hear her, and flips angrily through last week's *Toronto Stars* for evidence of the hair-eating animal.

"See the thanks I get for making Sunday lunch?" my grandmother says to my mother. "Every day it's the same thing. I get sick and tired of it. One day I'm gonna quit cooking for good."

"Take it easy, Ma," my mother says. "Remember what the doctor said."

Baldness has always been a contentious issue in my family. The hair-eating animal is a recent addition to the arsenal of explanations my grandfather habitually keeps in reserve to explain excessive hair loss. He attributes baldness in different people to a variety of causes, depending on their temperament, the circumstances and his own prejudices toward them. My grandfather maintains that his brother Tony's baldness is not due to the sustained efforts of an invisible hair-eating animal, but rather that Tony's hairless head is the lamentable – but inevitable – consequence of smoking cigarettes. Similarly, my grandfather maintains that his own father's lack of hair occurred because he never went to church or because he ate too much watermelon (depending on whether he wants to portray his father as irreligious or gluttonous). Even my mother has her own theory of baldness, which she expresses infrequently but clings to nonetheless.

"Your hair is like a plant," she told me once when I was seven years old and refused to remove my Blue Jays cap before entering church. "If you cover it all the time with a hat, it will die and fall out. You have to let it breathe. Just look at your grandfather."

"It's true," said my grandfather, who was in the process of removing his fedora, and was never opposed to the invention of a new explanation of hair loss. "When I came over from the old country I had beautiful hair. But then I started working and wearing hats, and my hair fell out."

Even though I was only seven years old at the time, I had already been shown the pictures of my grandfather's beautiful hair. There are two pictures of it in existence. In the first picture my grandfather is two years old. He is sitting on his mother's knee in Montescaglioso, his home town in Italy. They both have beautiful, curly black hair. The second picture of my grandfather 's beautiful hair was taken when he was twenty. He had already been in Canada for three years. He was earning a living primarily in a picture-frame factory during the week, and secondarily by selling bananas on Saturdays in Kensington market, and by shaving the beards off the other twelve men who lived in the same boarding house as him on Sunday mornings. In the picture he is sitting uncomfortably with his legs pushed to the right and his head facing to the left. It is a stiff pose. A pose designed by a photographer to seem appropriate to a man who had only had his picture taken once before in his life. My grandfather's beautiful hair is slicked straight back in a way that makes him look like Rudolf Valentino.

"It has nothing to do with small animals that eat the hair," I say to my grandfather, who is still rummaging though the papers in the laundry room. "Baldness is a matter of genetics."

My grandfather momentarily ceases looking through last week's papers and looks at me.

"The gene that causes baldness is passed matriarchally," I tell him. "It's something that's decided when you're born. You have nothing to do with it."

My grandfather looks at me sadly. Unlike most grandparents who find themselves alienated from their grandchildren by radical haircuts and unhinging music, my grandfather seems to regard gene expression for alopecia as the emblem of the generation gap. "You'll see," he tells me, and returns to last week's news.

I look at my mother for moral support.

"I'm staying out of this," she says. "When your grandfather has made up his mind, he's made up his mind."

My mother is making the salad at the kitchen counter. She sprinkles some wine vinegar onto the lettuce, tosses it and tastes it. Holding a piece of lettuce in her mouth, she sucks on it for a few seconds before she chews it up and swallows it. Then she shakes a little bit more vinegar into the bowl, tosses the salad and tastes it again. I know that the routine of sprinkling, tossing and tasting will continue until she thinks she has the ingredients mixed just right. Then she will ask my grandmother to come over and taste it.

"Hey, Mom," she says finally. "Come and taste the salad."

My grandmother puts down the wooden spoon with which she had been stirring the pot of linguini, and walks slowly across the kitchen. She randomly selects a leaf from the bowl and eats it. "Perfect," she tells my mother. "No one makes a salad like my Maria."

My grandmother walks slowly back to the stove. She stirs the pot slowly for a few minutes and then slowly extracts a single strand of linguini from the pot and runs it under some cold water. When it is cold enough, she puts it into her mouth and chews it slowly.

"Perfect," she says. "*Al dente.* Take them out."

That my grandmother does everything slowly is not a choice of her own. There was a time when she did everything quickly. She has been forced to change her lifestyle.

Her heart attack happened about a year ago. My grandfather had just complained that the pasta was overcooked. My grandmother started yelling back at him: she was fed up; she was tired of him complaining; one day she was going to quit cooking for good. Suddenly, she was unable to catch her breath and collapsed face first into her plate of pasta before anyone knew what was happening. At the hospital, the doctor said that she had suffered a "subendocardial myocardial infarction" and that she would have to change her lifestyle.

"Your grandfather just left," she told me once when I came to visit her in the hospital. "He was supposed to come this morning, but he only got here a couple of hours ago."

"What took him so long?" I asked.

"He left early enough," she said. "But he had trouble on the subway. He said he wasn't sure where to get off."

Later that evening I called my grandfather. "I hear you got lost on the subway today," I told him.

"I don't get lost on the subway," he replied. "I've been taking the subway longer than you've been alive."

My grandmother turns off the burner and takes the pot off the stove. She motions to me to come over to the counter. I lift up the pot and pour the contents into the strainer that is sitting in the kitchen sink. As I pour out the boiling water, steam rises into my face and clouds my glasses. When the pasta is all out of the pot, I put it back on the stove.

"What a strong boy I got," my grandmother says, giving me a little pinch on the cheek. "What a good boy."

"I hope this isn't overcooked," says my grandfather as my grandmother sets the pasta down on the table. He says this because he knows it is exactly what will make my grandmother angry.

"Do you hear that?" says my grandmother, to no one in particular. "That is what I have to put up with. That is what I get for making lunch. I get sick of it. Sometimes I just get fed up. If you don't watch, I'm going to quit cooking."

"Take it easy, Ma," says my mother. "Remember what the doctor said."

Ever since the heart attack, we get worried whenever my grandmother raises her voice. The doctor at the hospital told us that the next time she falls down face first into her pasta, it will probably be for the last time. She has been told to change her lifestyle. She has been told to take her medicine regularly. She has been told to take salt out of her diet. She has been told to stop yelling. She has been told not to get excited. It is for her own good.

My grandfather tastes the first of the linguini. "Perfect," he says. "No one makes linguini like your grandmother."

"*Madonn...*" says my grandmother, preferring to ignore the fact that she has just received a compliment. "If you don't watch out, I'm gonna quit cooking."

They are having an old argument. It is the same argument they had last week. It is the same argument they had the week before that. It is the same argument that has been going on for as long as I can remember. It is a kind of programmed hostility that replaces the affection they must have once felt for each other. They are not really having an argument; they are just talking. They have been yelling at each other for so long they have forgotten how to do anything else. I wonder sometimes if my mother and father would interact in a similar manner if my father were still alive. My father was killed in a car accident by a drunk driver when I was three years old. Years later my mother showed me a newspaper clipping of the accident.

"That's his car," she said, carefully unfolding the yellowed newsprint and handing it to me. "Look at the mirror on the driver's side."

I looked closely at the black-and-white photo of a mangled Volkswagen crumpled up against a lamppost. I could barely make out a tattered piece of cloth hanging on the mirror.

"That's your father's scarf," she told me. "He was wearing it when he went to work that morning. When I saw it in the paper it just about killed me."

After she showed me the newspaper clipping, she folded it neatly and put it back in the drawer where she got it from. She is the kind of woman who decides what needs to be done, then does it.

"What is the name of the animal that eats the hair?" I ask my grandfather.

"I don't know," he says. "I just read about it. "

"What day was it in the *Star*?" my mother asks him. "Maybe I saw it too."

"I can't remember what day, but they found it in Newmarket. It was in the schools and ate all the kids' hair."

My mother explains her father's mistake. She has seen the article. In Newmarket, some children at one of the public schools became infected by a rare tropical parasite that attacks the roots of the hair and causes baldness. My mother describes the picture that accompanied the article of several kindergarten children touching their bald heads in wonder. Somehow my grandfather has got it into his head that he contracted the same parasite.

"I told you," my grandfather says to me. "I may be old, but I'm not that old. I can still tell what's what."

"You could have fooled me," says my grandmother.

"Never mind, Annie," he tells her. "You can all laugh at me if you want, but when I'm gone, you'll see that I was right about a lot of things."

"Here we go again," says my grandmother.

"What do you mean, here we go again?" grandfather asks her.

"Do you see what I have to put up with?" she says to my mother. "This is all I get, all day, every day. Sometimes I get fed up. I just get fed up."

"Take it easy, Ma," says my mother.

"What am I gonna do?" my grandfather asks us. "Not talk about it? I can't eat, I can't sleep, I can't piss, I can't have sex — what's the use of living?"

"This is all I get," my grandmother says. "I don't even want to talk about last Wednesday. I don't want to get into that."

"What happened last Wednesday?" asks my mother and looks at them both. "Did something happen last Wednesday that you're not telling me about?"

"Nothing happened," says my grandfather.

"You call that nothing?" my grandmother asks him. "Here I am scared to death for six hours and you call it nothing."

"What happened?" asks my mother a second time.

"Nothing happened," says my grandfather more softly. "I just forgot to call your mother."

"Where were you?" asks my mother. She is looking at him angrily. It is a look that I recognize. It is the stern look of a parent who wants to find out exactly what happened in her house while she was away.

"Go ahead then," my grandfather says. "Tell them. You want to tell them. You brought it up in the first place. Just tell them."

"Your father went out last Wednesday to buy some bananas," says my grandmother. "They were on sale at the Ferlisi Brothers for twenty-four cents, so I said go and pick up some and I'll make some banana cake. He was doing nothing, so I figured he would- n't mind. This was at ten. When he's not back by three, I start to get worried.

He gets here at five and says that he got lost."

"What happened, Dad?" asks my mother. "Did you get lost?"

"I don't get lost," replies my grandfather. "I've been driving these streets since before you were born."

"Then what took you so long?" asks my grandmother.

"I got shopping at Ferlisi Brothers, and I ran into Tony DiCamuto," explains my grandfather. "He said that his daughter is getting married and wanted to know if we wanted to come to the reception."

"Dad," says my mother, softly. "Tony DiCarnuto passed away last spring. We went to the funeral."

My grandfather looks at my mother. For a moment he looks like he is about to say something, but he thinks better of it and only sighs instead.

"Are you forgetting things again?" asks my mother. "If you are, then it is something we have to know about."

"He forgets everything," says my grandmother. "The other day he's downstairs for three hours. I go down to see what he's doing, and he's just sitting there. When I come down, he asks me where I put the hammer. I tell him that it's where it's always been: in his tool box. I have to show him the tool box."

"You're going to have to tell Dr. Fogel about this," says my mother. She is the kind of woman who decides what needs to be done, and does it. I know that she will start watching my grandfather very closely. He will not be allowed to go out alone. He will not be allowed to drive. He will not be allowed to eat the same foods. He will need to take special medication. He will have to change his lifestyle. It will be for his own good. We finish the meal in silence. At one point I try to tell a funny story about a student in one of my classes who went to the wrong exam, but no one wants to listen. When my grandfather finishes his pasta, he stands up slowly from the table and walks into the living room. He sits down in his favourite chair, a green Lazy Boy that he and my grandmother bought for half price at Honest Ed's Midnight Madness Extravaganza thirty-two years ago.

I walk over to see if my grandfather is all right. He has his eyes shut, but I can tell he is not sleeping.

"Can I get you anything?" I ask.

"No," he says. "I just need to rest."

I watch as my grandfather picks up a picture from the table next to his chair. It is a black-and-white photo in an old hand-carved frame. The photo is of a young man sitting awkwardly on a cheap wooden chair. I know which picture it is without looking at it.

"I had beautiful hair then," he says, and slowly puts the picture back on the table. He reaches for the remote and turns on the television. He leans back in the Lazy Boy and pretends to sleep. His bald head looks very small against the back of the chair.

TOWER

A

The first version of this story was written on the inside of a greeting card – a greeting card that had, on its front, a picture of a bride and groom holding hands under an archway of white roses. The inside of the card was left blank, and it was in that white space that I tried to write this story for the first time. I wanted to be eloquent and brief, but also to employ a form that was properly medieval; I produced an illuminated manuscript, the kind of document on which, a thousand years ago, it would not be uncommon for a scribe to write the adventures of King Arthur.

My illuminated manuscript consisted of just one, single word: CONGRATULATIONS. I covered the Ns with red roses and gold rings. I drew an overweight cherub hanging off the top of the S. I put stained-glass windows into the sides of each of the As, transforming both into tiny replicas of the church in which Gabriella and Professor Edward Theobald were going to be married. I extended the tops of the As so they were banging their steeples against the sky above them, which was blue.

(The sky is always blue in medieval illuminated manuscripts. This is because blue is the colour of God; or at least it used to be, in the Middle Ages. Medieval man believed in a blue heaven: that all of the angels, the saints, and even God himself, were blue.)

It was going to be perfect, an epistle that demonstrated my goodwill while it allowed me to avoid actually *saying* anything. But, as I was colouring the sky blue, I looked at the first A and saw it didn't look like a church at all. I saw I had extended the steeple too far.

It looked like a miniature CN Tower.

I tore the card up and threw it into the garbage. I thought I had given up trying to write this story. But then, three months later, I received a letter from Professor Edward Theobald, describing the wedding and telling me about Gabriella's great discovery, and I sat down to write this story a second time; this time, as a story.

(That there is nothing of real insight, of profound authenticity in these introductory comments, I know. They are not here to impress. They exist as a beginning. There is a beginning to everything.)

B

I don't need to know the details. I can imagine how, and who touched who first, but I don't need confirmation.

I found out about it in Washington. In the hotel room. I went out to buy cigarettes and had gotten down to the hotel lobby before realizing I had forgotten my wallet. I took the elevator back up and unlocked the door without knocking.

And that was when I saw them.

Professor Edward Theobald was sitting on the bed. Gab was on her knees in front of him.

The room was completely silent, almost.

He had his eyes closed. Neither of them saw me standing there. A few minutes later Professor Edward Theobald came.

She stood up to get a Kleenex from the table behind her, and that was when she saw me.

I use Professor Edward Theobald's title rather than his name because it is what he would have done. I never heard him refer to himself any other way. I have said his *title*, both out loud and inside my head, more than a thousand times. It has not worn away with use.

(As I type it now, I see him bending to shake my hand for the first time. Bending was a necessity for Professor Edward Theobald. He was slightly over seven feet tall. It is a perfect height, he often told people, for a professor of Medieval Literature – for a man who specializes in the study of dwarves and giants.)

C

I have a photograph of the three of us – Professor Edward Theobald, Gabriella Brooks, and myself – that was taken just hours before everything fell apart in that hotel room. It was taken at the Smithsonian, and the three of us are standing in front of a painting of a dead fish on a checkered tablecloth. I don't recall the name of the painting, but it must have made us laugh and that was why the picture was taken.

In the photo, Gabriella and I are twenty-seven. Professor Edward Theobald is sixty. He is holding in his hands a map of Washington and looking directly into the lens of the camera. But the flash has made him blink, and for that reason you cannot see the colour of his eyes, which are blue. His silver hair is freshly slicked back – shining with a brilliance known as Brylcreem – combed in a style that was out of style before Gabriella and I were born.

That morning I watched Professor Edward Theobald slick back his hair in the hotel room the three of us were sharing. He had just gotten out of the shower and was sitting on the bed in a grey undershirt. I remember him taking the container out of his suitcase and putting his elongated fingers into it, rubbing it into his bony hands and then into his hair, pushing it backwards so it was flat against his skull. Then he put on his shirt. Gabriella walked over to the bed and laid her hand on his head. I love the way that feels, she said and smiled, like she was joking.

D

My dissertation (still incomplete) was about a character named Kay, a talkative and generally annoying Knight of the Round Table. Despite his relative unimportance in the legend as a whole, he makes an appearance in every surviving story about King Arthur.

Kay is the Doubting Thomas of the Round Table. There is a moment, right at the beginning of each story, when Kay speaks up louder than all the other knights, and either recommends that they ignore the crisis at hand because it doesn't concern them, or suggests that it would be more prudent to avoid a battle because they could lose it. Kay uses different words in each story, but always says the same thing – that the adventure that is about to happen will not happen.

Kay, of course, is always wrong. The adventure always happens; if there were no adventure there would be no story. But while most critics regard Kay as an essentially dislikable and very minor character, I see him as an integral part of the legend. I argue in my dissertation that Kay's presence in the stories increases the credibility of the stories, as stories – that there has to be someone at the beginning of each story who thinks that it is not a story at all.

Kay is always that person: the only Knight of the Round Table who consistently ignores the fact that he is a character in the Arthurian myth. The rest of the Knights seem to know it (whenever Sir Gawain, for example, defeats an evil knight, he always thinks about the story that will be told about the victory rather than the victory itself), but Kay is the exception. He never wants to go to war. He never wants to save any maidens. He always wants to finish his meal. He never knows he is a character in a story. Either that, or he thinks he is in an entirely different kind of story. A story about himself perhaps.

E

Medieval Literature, according to Professor Edward Theobald, is the kind of literature that no one hates to read. You always know the ending. You always know the beginning. But the beginning and the ending aren't important. What matters is the middle. The study of Medieval Literature, according to Professor Edward Theobald, is the study of the stories that everyone knows without knowing that they know them.

I met him on my second day at the University of Toronto. I was in the library, looking for the place where I was supposed to get my picture taken for my library card, but instead of finding the photographer I found a book. I chose the book randomly, from the stacks, in the hope that the author, or perhaps even the call number, might provide me with some clue as to where I was. It was then that I noticed Professor Edward Theobald standing next to me, looking at the book in my hands. It was *The Art of Courtly Love* by Andreas Capellanus.

"An excellent choice," he said. "I recall reading it for the first time when I was about your age." I nodded. "My name is Professor Edward Theobald," he continued, folding himself in two in order to shake my hand. "And you – if I might hazard a guess – are an undergraduate."

"Paul Pellazari," I told him.

And we stood there. I turned over the old book in my hands and Professor Edward Theobald stroked his beard.

(The truth is that Professor Edward Theobald was not – and is not now – a handsome man. His hair, even ten years ago, was completely grey. He had it slicked back on his head and tucked behind his ears. His beard, which was untrimmed and ungainly, was a fading shade of red. His eyelashes, which were white, were almost non-existent, and his eyes bulged out of his head so insistently that I had trouble imagining him ever sleeping. His hands were bloodless and bony, and resembled my idea of what a dead man's hands should look like. I remember noticing his right hand particularly, because, as he looked at me, he used it to stroke his beard, as if there were a small furry animal that had attached itself to his face which he was trying to tame.)

"I'm an English major," I said, and before I had finished speaking, he had snatched the timetable from my hands, considering it carefully before handing it back to me. I noticed that the paper was moist where he had touched it, and I resisted the urge to wipe it clean.

"Drop that course," he said, pointing at the Drama course I was going to take. "Instead, come to my course on Medieval Literature."

From somewhere within the folds of his huge jacket he produced a fountain pen, scribbled the information down on my timetable, and before I could say anything he was gone. His huge legs took him to the other side of the library, and out of earshot, in a matter of seconds.

I went to the first class.

There were about ten other students there. It was my first day, before I knew anyone at the University, and I remember sitting alone, near the back, watching the other students talk to each other, when the room became suddenly silent.

Professor Theobald Edward had started to speak.

He was reading a list. I discovered later that he began every year of classes by reading the same list, softly at first, but getting steadily louder until he was banging his fist on his desk and shouting.

"Jousts. Falcons. Vendettas. Malice. True love. Ghosts. Wizards. Nefarious knights. Magnificent princesses" – he was getting louder – "Brave princes. Ugly stepmothers. Death. Revenge. Fearless exploits. Ingenious design. Magic. Castles. Magic. Snakes. Love" – by this time he had reached full volume – "Justice. Deadly Plagues. Blessings. Giants."

I knew then that I wanted to be an English major; that I wanted to be a professor of Medieval Literature; in short, that I wanted to be Professor Edward Theobald.

F

Fredericton is not a bad place to live. I work here in the university library, a job I got through Geoffrey Booth, the president of the university, a former medievalist – a man to whom I was introduced by Professor Edward Theobald. I called him from Toronto and said that I was taking a leave of absence from the Graduate Program and moving to the east coast, and he pulled some strings. He didn't ask any questions.

(Every two months or so, Geoffrey Booth and I get together in the faculty lounge to talk about the state of Arthurian criticism and why none of the new undergraduates takes his course on the subject. Geoffrey Booth's theory is that the lack of interest in the Middle Ages is directly related to the ascendancy of Beavis and Butthead.)

Most of the other librarians here tell each other that they will be working at the library for only few years. With me it is different. My visions of professorship have faded and the library has become a way of life. I have grown accustomed to a methodical existence: a life of many days but few events. I am awake by eight, at work by nine, at home by six, and asleep by twelve. I order pizza on Fridays. Sometimes I go out for a beer with my fellow librarians, but not often. I suspect working in the library has had something to do with this routine lifestyle: persistent alphabetization makes for an orderly and ordered existence.

G

Name: Gabriella Brooks
   Height: 5 feet 5 inches
   Born: June 4, 1964
   Birthplace: Aurora, Ontario, Canada (suburb of Toronto)
   Eyes: Brown
   Shoe Size: Seven
   Hair: Black (with red highlights)
   Favourite Colour: Blue
   Occupation: Astronomy student
   Favourite Things: heavy maple furniture, Marianne Faithful, aerobics, red wine, candles, playing the flute, Joni Mitchell,

being kissed on the ear, terrycloth bathrobes, Vivaldi, African violets, Shetland ponies, Sean Connery, and strawberry lip gloss.

Sometimes I would call her Gabbie but most of the time it was Gab. When she was nine years old she hated her name, she said that "Gab" sounded like the name of a goat. Professor Edward Theobald never called her anything other than Gabriella. Apparently, that now is what she insists on being called. People, as everyone knows, can be made by their names: call anyone a Gabriella and they become a Gabriella, call anyone a Professor Edward Theobald and they become a Professor Edward Theobald. The name is a sound that sticks.

I say her name as I type it and I notice (in a way I never noticed when I said her name every day, when it never meant anything, when I could say it to her) that my mouth has to become quite flexible when it is speaking her name – wide at the beginning to say the first A and then narrow at the end to complete the articulation. Gabriella. She was named, her mother told me, after an angel. Gabriella. The word remains, for me, a beautiful and mysterious sound. Even today, even after the fucking hell she put me through.

H

I have read somewhere that about eighty percent of married people who go to university marry the people they date there. Gab and I were going to be part of that eighty percent. At least that was what I thought.

We met at the University of Toronto in our first year. But it wasn't until the middle of second year that we became a couple. It happened during a party in our residence. I was drunk and she was drunk and we went back to my room. I wish the details were exceptional: that I had brushed her cheek in a certain way or whispered her name with magic results or rescued her from the clutches of a sexually frustrated leper, but it wasn't like that. We went back to my room and we both knew what would happen next. It was like saying the alphabet.

Two years after that, when we had both finished our undergraduate degrees, we realized that we had to move out of residence.

We had both applied to the Graduate Program, but didn't know if we would be accepted. We had to find somewhere to live for the summer; I wanted us to move in together. We had talked about it before, but never seriously. Gab always seemed unsure about it being the right thing to do. It seemed like such a big step, she said, the step you take before getting married. I avoided asking her until one night when I took her out for dinner to celebrate our second anniversary of seeing each other.

We went to the restaurant atop the CN Tower; it was Gab's favourite restaurant. Whenever she had something to celebrate – the end of a school year, the beginning of a school year, a good mark on a paper – that's where she went. She had the chicken and I had the steak, and then I asked her. She said that she didn't see why not. Those were her words, exactly: "I don't see why not."

And we had nothing more to say. I looked into my coffee and Gab looked out at the city, and then she said what she always said whenever we ate dinner at the restaurant at the top of the CN Tower.

"A perfect view. The only place in Toronto where you can't see the CN Tower."

That summer we moved in together and were informed we had both been accepted into the Graduate Program at the

University of Toronto: she in Astronomy and myself in English. We lived in a one-bedroom on the main floor of a house on Robert Street, my desk in the kitchen and hers in the living room. There were so many books that they had to be stacked on the floor. Her parents gave her a futon as a graduation present, and I took some old furniture from my parents' basement. We bought a coffee maker and microwave oven and a kitchen table. And that was our home.

I

I am now thirty-one. Older than Keats was when he died. When I was an undergraduate, I thought I was Keats. I believed I would die young and leave behind a beautiful corpse, a handful of irreproachable poems, and a suitcase full of immaculately written love letters. As long as you are younger than Keats, you are allowed to believe that.

I once imagined that this story, or something like it, would be my perfect poem. I had visions of Gabriella unwrapping a copy of it after my death (as the proviso in my will dictated), of her sad eyes travelling across my troubled pages, of her persuading Professor Edward Theobald to give up the study of Medieval Literature and devote himself to the editing of my correspondence, and of Gabriella's subsequent withdrawal into a convent. But that's not what happened. This remains unpublished and I am still alive; the arc of my life has remained resolutely suburban.

J

J is a hook.

According to Andreas Capellanus who wrote *The Art of Courtly Love* in 1458, the word for love comes from the word for hook:

Love gets its name (*amor*) from the word for hook (*amus*), which means "to capture" or "to be captured," for he who is in love is captured in the chains of desire and wishes to capture someone else with his hook. Just as a skillful fisherman tries to attract fishes by his bait and to capture them on his crooked hook, so the man who is a captive of love tries to attract another person by his allurements and exerts all his efforts to unite two different hearts with an intangible bond, or if they are already united he tries to keep them so forever (31).

This passage is at the beginning of the book. After he has defined love – "a certain inborn suffering derived from the sight of an excessive meditation upon the beauty of the opposite sex" – Capellanus proceeds to discuss what it means to be in love, and how to stay in love. Or more accurately, how to *keep* someone in love with you. The way to do this, apparently, is through an effective use of pick-up lines. In the pages that follow, Capellanus provides his readers with a series of dialogues between a man and a woman that illustrate the effective (or ineffective) use of a pick-up line. These pick-up lines, of course, are not supposed to be used in order to gain new lovers but to keep the old ones (there is always *more* than one, at least in the Middle Ages).

The first time that Professor Edward Theobald met Gabriella was during my first year in the Ph.D. program. Gab and I were walking across campus one day and we happened to meet him.

I made the introductions and they shook hands. I stood there and watched while Professor Edward Theobald unfolded his five skeletal fingers and saw Gabriella's hand disappear into his. And then he bent himself slowly in two, bringing her hand to his lips.

"You are a jewel," he told her.

We stood there talking, and I noticed that he did not let go of her hand after he had kissed it. He stood there, touching her, and it looked like his fingers had somehow dug themselves into her skin.

K

Gab was, according to her Roman Catholic mother, named after an angel. But she didn't act like an angel, and she certainly didn't look like one.

She was, and still is, quite striking. With her high heels on, she is a whole head taller than I, with long black hair that hangs down below her shoulders, and blue eyes. She has a small, angular nose, and red lips that can frown with a petulance or smile with an arrogance that can only be described as queenly. Her complexion is perfect; in the six years we lived together I never saw – even in the midst of exams and the flu – her perfect skin marred by a single blemish. But really, it was her voice that made me want her most. I loved to listen to her exchange equations with fellow Astronomy students on the telephone. There was no number, no algebraic symbol, no mathematical operation which her marvellous voice could not cloak in an air of innuendo and mystery.

There had been a time, at the very beginning, when she told me everything about each of her lovers. The first had been Ralph Moyle, he was nineteen and she was seventeen. She lost her virginity in his car while it was parked behind a bowling alley and while Led Zeppelin played on the radio. Then Thomas Seeber, a boy in her own grade, two weeks after breaking up with Ralph (he was moving away, going to university). But she hadn't slept with Thomas, she had only sucked his dick, and he had come in her mouth. It tasted like chickpeas, she told me, like hummus before you put the spices in. Then it was eighteen-year-old Joseph Franchetto, after a high-school dance when she had been drinking. She went out with Joseph Franchetto for a year; but it came to an end when people found out she had also been sleeping with a twenty-year-old mechanic named Brian Spiers, who worked in a gas station down the street from the school. Someone had seen her walk into the garage and the whole thing came out. The mechanic, she said, wasn't the smartest person in the world but he could fuck you like a gorilla – no doubt to compensate. She thought she was in love with him, and let him take her from behind. That hurt, she told me. I won't do it again.

She told me each of their names, going into the most minute detail, and I would laugh and listen in the dark while she described each of her lovers. How they touched her. How they looked when they came. I thought her absolute confidence was her way of letting me know how much I was worth, that I was more valuable than all of the rest.

We would talk about our fantasies, about the people we knew and wanted. They had to be people we knew; people from the movies or magazines didn't count. Those were the conversations that always ended with us fighting. I remember one in particular, just before everything fell apart.

"Sometimes," she said, "I think about that professor of yours, the tall one. Look at his fingers and feet, they're so long – I wonder if the rest of him is like that."

"He's an old man," I said. "You'd kill him."

"No, I mean it," she continued. "Did you see the way he held my hand the other day, I mean there is a power to him, a kind of energy you feel whenever you touch him. He has such – presence."

"Then why don't you go live with him, if you want him so badly." I rolled over. I felt like someone had put a knife into my side.

"Are you crazy?" she said, her fingers on my shoulder. "I'm joking, it was just a joke. He's repulsive – it was disgusting the way he wouldn't let go of my hand the other day. I'm joking, come on."

"Of course you're joking," I said. "I can't believe you thought I was serious about you being serious." I lay there, staring at the ceiling like an astronomer whose telescope is a mystery to him, a telescope that is either entirely imprecise or impossibly acute, and I turned around in the bed to look at her.

L

Professor Edward Theobald's famous book is called *The Lost Lancelot: A Cultural Archetype Re-examined*. He wrote it more than thirty years ago as his dissertation at the University of Birmingham, and it remains a central text for anyone interested in the subject. After the publication of the book, he was offered a full professorship at the University of Toronto. He was only thirty-one years old – the youngest full professor in the history of any Canadian university.

The Lost Lancelot is a translation and analysis of a seventy-nine-page document known now as *The Theobald Manuscript*, which is actually the earliest version of the Lancelot myth. It is a manuscript which Professor Edward Theobald discovered in the basement of a library in Birmingham when he was twenty-six years old and just beginning his Ph.D. In the introduction to *The Lost Lancelot*, he describes, in a typical melodramatic manner, how he discovered the manuscript:

I remember quite clearly my discovery of *The Theobald Manuscript* in the library that day and what I remember is, at first, that I was attracted by the colours on the page. It is an illuminated manuscript, and the illustrations are profuse – the letters are covered in red roses and gold rings, there are plump cherubs hanging off the tails of each S, and every A on the page has been made into a church with a blue sky above it. It was not until later, after I had begun to translate it, that I understood what I had found. Paleographic evidence suggests that the scribe who produced the manuscript lived in approximately 900 AD, more than two hundred years, of course, before the birth of Chretien de Troyes, whose *Le Chevalier de la Charrette* is commonly regarded as the first mention of Lancelot...

The Theobald Manuscript is an important discovery because it suggests it is only in the later versions of the Arthurian legend that Lancelot is a sympathetic character – the young, handsome lover, the strongest Knight of the Round Table who is flawed only by his illicit love for Queen Guinevere. In all of the later versions of the story, from Mallory to Mary Stewart, Lancelot ultimately achieves redemption by repentance and by triumphing over his lust.

In *The Theobald Manuscript*, Lancelot is pathetic. The poem begins with Lancelot falling in love with Guinevere, but she refuses to love him back. In response, Lancelot kidnaps her and places her in a tower, refusing to let her go until she agrees to fall in love with him. Which, of course, she does. She is then res-cued by Arthur, whom she no longer loves. He puts her in his own tower, a tower designed specifically to exclude Lancelot.

And that is where the poem *almost* ends.

The final two hundred lines of *The Theobald Manuscript* describe Lancelot's return to England from the Holy Land, an old man forced to come back without the Grail. The poet describes Lancelot's armour hanging loosely around his old shoulders. His horse is standing beside him, bleeding. Lancelot is looking at the castle where Edward awaits him and the tower where Guinevere is imprisoned, and he knows that if he returns without the Grail, he will be put to death. All the same, he gets back on his horse and begins to ride. That is where *The Theobald Manuscript* ends.

M

Most people think that M is the middle letter of the alphabet. That is not the case. The truth is that there is no middle to the alphabet. The middle of the alphabet happens when no one is looking, too quickly for any letter. In the same way we say hello and we say goodbye, not really knowing the difference.

One day I went to have a meeting with Professor Edward Theobald about my dissertation. I got there early and saw the door of his office was closed. I knew he was in there because the light was on. I sat down outside the office and waited. Seconds later the door opened and Gabriella walked out.

"What are you doing here?" I asked her.

"Edward gave me a call," she said. "He's working on a paper that involves some astronomical history, and asked if I would read it."

"Edward?" I asked her.

She looked at me.

"I mean, you call him Edward."

"Of course," she said. "What do you call him?"

"How come you didn't tell me – what are you doing sneaking around?"

"I'm not sneaking around," she said. "He called me today, and I came over."

It was then that Professor Edward Theobald came into the hallway. "Children," he said, "please keep your voices down – there is learning going on, at this very minute, in these hallways."

Gabriella laughed. I didn't. She stopped.

"We can talk about this at home," said Gab.

"That's a splendid idea," said Professor Edward Theobald. "But right now we must enter the office and discuss the infinite dissertation, a dissertation about the margins of a margin."

He motioned me into his office. The two of them laughed, again.

N

While working on the article, Gab started spending a lot of time with Professor Edward Theobald. She would go to his office at least once a day, and said the article had something to do with the stars that would have been in the sky at the time of King Arthur's birth. She was never explicit, which made me suspicious, because she could have been – it was my field, after all, not hers. Gab would be co-author; it would be a major step in her career. It didn't bother me. Which was not entirely true. I kept thinking of the conversation we'd had that night, and I found myself walking by Professor Edward Theobald's office when I knew he wasn't expecting me, when I knew Gab was there. I never saw anything. In fact, when they noticed me lurking outside, I was always invited in. They were always civil. More than civil, really, they were kind. I began to think they felt sorry for me. I thought this had something to do with my inability to complete my dissertation and the way my academic career had been grinding to a slow halt while Gab's was taking off. I would look at Professor Edward Theobald, a serene academic presence behind his oak desk, and I would think of Gab's story about cheating on poor eighteen-year-old Joseph Franchetto. She said that each time she saw the unsuspecting Joseph after fucking that mechanic, she felt a greater love for him; or at least a genuine sympathy. And I would see Gab, looking at me with her understanding eyes, and I would worry.

I don't remember whose idea it was that I go with them to Washington; I remember Gabriella telling me about the trip, but I think it was Professor Edward Theobald who suggested that I come along, to share the driving. It was his idea.

"O," she said, when she saw me standing there, in the hotel room.

Round like a hole. A letter with its inside cut out. When you say it your mouth thinks it is kissing something. Or screaming. I walked over to the window and looked out and tried not to watch Professor Edward Theobald push his old penis into his pants. He didn't look at me. He stood up and left the room without a word. Gabriella came over to the window and I pushed her away. She fell against the bed and hit her face on the night table. For a moment I thought I had really hurt her. But it was only her nose that was bleeding. I picked up the box of Kleenex from the bed and handed it to her. She knocked it out of my hand and she ran out of the room, slamming the door behind her.

"O," I said, to the empty room, looking at the used Kleenex on the floor, one of which was covered with her blood.

I packed my things and took a cab to the bus station. I came back to Toronto. That was the second last time I saw her. This chapter is about all the things you never think will happen to you even when you are having them happen, even after they have happened. Everyone, really, is the Kay in the story of his own life.

P

One of the first things I did when I got back to Toronto was have my film developed. I wasn't sure why then; but it seems plain now that I was looking for some kind of evidence, some sign I somehow missed. The film had the photo of the three of us at the Smithsonian. In that photograph I am looking at her. At the red in her black hair. I was always confounded by that redness, by how anything that black could be so red at the same time it was black. In the photo, she is looking at him – her hand is touching mine but she is looking at him.

Q

After getting back to Toronto, I tried to be an alcoholic. I went to the liquor store to stock up, and came back with so many bottles I had to take a cab home. Having bought booze made me feel better, like I was doing something real.

I started drinking. First the vodka, mixing it with tomato juice. Then I switched to rum. Straight. Pretty soon I couldn't sit up straight. I began drinking water. And then I started getting sick. It lasted for about a day and a half. I knelt in front of the toilet and swore I would never drink again, and it was during that time in the washroom that I noticed the magazine rack. I pulled out a magazine and saw it was a copy of *Cosmopolitan* that Gab had bought about a year ago.

I opened it to a page with a completed questionnaire, a number of questions which women were supposed to ask themselves before marrying their boyfriends:

1. You come from similar backgrounds.
2. He holds your hand when you're out with friends.
3. The two of you have every single interest in common.
4. You don't like the relationship he has with his mother.
5. You're the first girlfriend he hasn't cheated on.
6. You enjoy watching the way he eats with chopsticks.
7. Your early courtship was laced with coincidences.
8. Talking is rare during lovemaking.
9. You love it when his toes touch yours in bed.
10. You can't wait to get married, so you can change his bad habits.

It's the kind of thing that appears all the time in *Cosmopolitan*. But what made this questionnaire different was that in order for a girl to be sure she should marry her boyfriend she was supposed to answer half of the questions true and half of them as false. It is a level of complexity rare in the pages of *Cosmopolitan*.

The thing was: Gab had done this.

She has filled out the questionnaire exactly right: five false and five true. There was no question to who she should have married.

R

I avoided the university for a month. I called in sick and cancelled my classes. People thought I was dying. Finally Professor
Edward Theobald called me. He said Gab wanted to know what
would be a good time for her to come and collect her things.

"Anytime," I said. "Just let me know when she's coming and
I'll make sure I'm here."

"That is precisely what I am trying to avoid," he told me.
"Gabriella has asked me to inquire when you won't be there. She
does not want to see you."

"That's understandable," I said. "But I think you can also see
my point."

"Your point?"

"That if there is going to be any cock sucking on the prem-
ises, I will have to insist on chaperoning."

"Vulgarity doesn't become you," he told me. "And please,
don't make this more difficult than it already is – no one is enjoying this."

"Come off it," I said. "I can't believe you steal her from me
and then take this high moral tone."

"May I remind you – and please, don't interpret this as my
taking a high moral tone, as you put it – that Gabriella chose me
over you. No one forced her to do anything. If you think about
it, you'll see that it's not really me who you are angry at, but yourself."

"It was you in that hotel room!"

"I'm not denying that," he said slowly. He spoke calmly, in a
voice I had heard before. It was his lecture voice. He was speaking like he was giving a lesson in pronunciation, like he was
reading a list. "But if it had not been me," he went on, "it would
have been someone else. You are not angry at me. You are angry

141

at the world. At a world in which Gabriella Brooks no longer loves you."

For a moment I didn't know what to say. Then I asked him the question I had been asking myself since that day in the Washington hotel room: "How long?" I asked. "When did it start?"

"I don't want to be having this conversation," said Professor Edward Theobald.

"Did it begin that day when I saw you together at the office? Did you fuck her on your desk, Edward? Did she suck your dick there, while you were reading my dissertation? Did you fuck her *on...*"

"I don't want to be having this conversation," he said again, this time more forcefully, cutting me off. "This is precisely why Gabriella does not want to have an encounter with you when she removes her belongings from your apartment. If you are there, you will have a similar kind of outburst. And you will say things you will regret later – such an emotional confrontation will be no good for anyone."

"I think it would be good," I told him. "I think it would make me feel a lot better."

"I am hanging up the phone now," he said. "We will be over tomorrow at two. Please do not be there."

S

The next day I hid in the bushes across the street from the house and waited for them. I had to sit there for more than half an hour before they arrived.

When they did, Professor Edward Theobald was with her, and he helped her carry things out of the house. The last thing

142

they took was her futon. It was awkward but not heavy; they manoeuvred it out to the porch and then stopped to rest. After a couple of seconds they went to pick it up again. Gab tripped and fell forward. Professor Edward Theobald was also thrown off balance. They both fell onto the futon and their heads hit. Not hard, but hard enough to surprise them both. They both laughed and I watched them kissing on the futon, his fingertips moving like bony snakes across her blouse. I wished, desperately, for it to rain. But the sun was shining and the sky was blue.

T

The CN Tower is listed in the *Guinness Book of World Records* as the tallest free-standing structure in the world. It is one thousand eight hundred twenty-two feet and one inch tall. It took thirty tons of concrete to complete. The maximum sway is three feet at the very top of its antenna. There is a restaurant at the one thousand one hundred and forty-foot level. People call it the Top of Toronto. The tower has the world's longest concrete staircase with two thousand five hundred and seventy steps. Lightning strikes the tower approximately two hundred times a year. No one has ever jumped off it and killed themselves. William Eustace had parachuted out of the restaurant in 1983, survived, and was arrested immediately after. He still lives in Toronto and is employed by the Post Office. On a clear day, the CN tower is visible from a one hundred and nine mile radius.

U

These are the things Gabriella leaves behind in the apartment: one ten-inch frying pan, one spatula, one used calculator battery, one broken digital watch, seven issues of *The Planetary Report*, one issue of *Cosmopolitan*, two umbrellas (one red, one black), *Thermal Physics* (with her name, and my address, written on the inside cover in blue ink), five birthday cards (from her Uncle George, her mother, her grandmother, her best friend Julie, and from myself), two unopened packages of graph paper, an almost empty container of Secret underarm deodorant, seven hair elastics, two unused tampons, and a single pair of white underwear with pink roses on them and a blue bow stitched into the front.

The day after she removed her things from the apartment, I put these things in a garbage can in the middle of my kitchen, and went down to the variety store. I bought some lighter fluid.

The fire lasted less than five minutes. Then I took the blackened remains and put them in a manila envelope and walked down to the University of Toronto. I walked into University College and put them in Professor Edward Theobald's mailbox.

I think I might have gotten to the end of the hallway before I turned around and retrieved the envelope.

That u-turn is its own kind of cowardice. I took the envelope out of his mailbox and started walking home. On the way I stopped and started walking back to the university, determined to put it into Professor Edward Theobald's hands myself; but then I changed my mind and turned around again. I did that for about an hour. Eventually I got back to my apartment with the envelope still in my hands, and dropped it into the garbage.

I started seeing Gabriella everywhere. Or at least I thought it was her. The first time I was walking down Bloor Street and I thought I saw her through the window of Future's Bakery. But it was only her hands. From a distance it looked like it was her, but then I went into the bakery, and saw that it was a completely different woman. Only her hands were right. I walked straight out of there.

That went on for about a month, and when I wasn't seeing her, I was seeing the CN Tower. There is no one in Toronto who does not look at the CN Tower at least once a day. Even in the middle of the night you can see it. There are two lights at the top of it that blink twenty-four hours a day as a reminder of its continued existence. I began to see the terrible thing she had done by leaving me in our apartment, in our city, alone. I was the one who had wanted to move in together, after all. I was the one who had not wanted to leave Toronto and go to a different university. Therefore I inherited both the apartment and the city, and it became a terrible thing to look out the window and see the CN Tower.

I knew I had to get out of that apartment and out of Toronto. I needed a vacation. I withdrew from the Graduate Program and packed my things. I sold my books and furniture and came here to Fredericton. It had been less than two months since our trip to Washington.

W

Not long after I moved to Fredericton, I received a letter from Professor Edward Theobald. As usual, it was typed. He prefers to type because it is faster than writing by hand, but he will only type certain words – those he cannot abbreviate. His letter to me was in the same illogically abbreviated style that he writes everything, and its parapraxic errata brought back the terrible business one more time. I reproduce it here:

Dear Paul,

I cn only assme you stl harbor a crtn degree of resentment twds myself & my fiancée.

That's rht – my *fiancée*. Gabriella & I are going to be married and we wld like you to come to the wding. Pls find enclosed an invitation & let us know whn you will be arving. You can stay at our place if you like. There is alwys a rm for you there.

You are nvr far frm our thghts. You know from our ltrs (which you didn't write bck to!) tht we wr distrssd to hear of your withdrwl from the Graduate Program. We wish you wld cnsr rtning to cmplt your thesis. You owe it to yrself to finish what you've strtd. I suppose your withdrwl from the prgm is to be exptd. I have not tkn it personally. I mention again my offer to do my upmost to assist you should you want to return & use all of my influence to help you over any admst hurdles.

You are prbly still angry. I undst that anger. But I cnsdr where that anger is coming from. You sd I "stole" Gabriella. It pained me to hr tht, because thr was a time when you wr my friend. Whn I ws wth Gabriella I was not thinking about being your friend. Tht mch is true. I was not thinking about you. It had nothing to do with you.

Thr is only G. Thr is nothing else.

Thgs are going well for G., in tht the oth ngt, she ws tking some routine slides of the ngt sky, and noticed a bright smuge in th lft hd comer of the frame. Tned out to be a comet, that only 1 oth astronomer dctmented, and sh'll gt partial credit for the discvery. Hpe ths lttr fds you well. We hrd you are wrking in the Fredericton lbry; bt is all we know. G., as evr, snds her regards. Fnd enclosed an invitation, and plse, try to attend.

Yours,

Professor Edward Theobald

Of course, I didn't go to the wedding. But on the day it happened, I went out and bought a greeting card that had a picture of a bride and a groom on its front holding hands under an archway of white roses. It was on the inside of that card that I tried to write this story for the first time.

X

After the wedding, I decided to call her. She was living with Professor Edward Theobald so I didn't have to look up the number. I don't know what I would have done if he had picked up the phone. I supposed I was ready, poised, to hang up. But I didn't have to.

I could tell she was surprised. We talked about nothing. We talked about the weather, about the fact that the Blue Jays might win the World Series for the third time, and about her discovery of the comet. It was going to be named the Brooks-Cobb comet, because a British astronomer named Cobb had also noticed its appearance in the sky. It struck me as terribly poetic to have something in the sky named after oneself, I thought, and I told her so.

"It's not such a big deal," she told me. "When you discover a comet you don't really have to do anything – you just have to be looking in the right place at the right time. Everyone has a comet pass over them at one time or another – the trick is to notice it.

My comet will be back in another five hundred and seventy-two years, they come and go."

Y

Y is a letter that needs no extrapolation. It stands for itself. Y is composed of one upward stroke of the pen that suddenly become two. Like one road that suddenly becomes split. There is no going straight with the Y. The Y either goes to the right or to the left. If the Y went straight it wouldn't be a Y. It would be an I. An I is a Y in which everything worked out. You need both letters in the alphabet.

Z

So what can you do? One thing: you build a tower. The tower never works. You knock down the tower. You tell a story about the tower not working. About a woman who does not stay in her tower and the tragedy that happens to her and her lover. Or: you tell a story that is itself a tower. But not a tower that keeps anyone prisoner. A story like the CN Tower, a tower in which no one can live, but everyone can see. This is the story of Professor Edward Theobald's and Gabriella Brooks's life together. The story of their falling in love. The story of their love. It is the story that lies forever and for good at the centre of their lives. I am the protagonist, the central character, the hero. They are characters in a story about me.

AUGUST 7, 1921

After ten years of "Give-Away Days," the Yankees had managed to dole out a greater variety of baseball paraphernalia than any other team in the history of baseball. The first Give-Away Day was on June 3, 1918 (when 6,500 Yankee caps were given away), and the last was on September 17, 1927 (when over 80,000 pretzels shaped like Yankee logos were distributed). In between, there had been Cap Day, Bottle Opener Day, Pennant Day, Cigar Day, Pillow Day, Sock Day, Mug Day, Pretzel Day, Jersey Day, Sneaker Day, Baseball Card Day, Camera Day, Hot Dog Day, Tobacco Day, Chewing Tobacco Day, Cracker Jack Day, and Peanut Day, to name a few.

August 7, 1921, was Bat Day.

According to *The Completely Complete Book of Baseball Statistics* by Dr. Venus Guzman, there were 21,106 paying customers in Yankee Stadium that day, and 15,000 of them had been given complimentary baseball bats as they entered the stadium. This story is concerned with seven of those people. The first two are Mary and Lyman Labrow.

I know about the Labrows thanks to an article published on September 21, 1923 (roughly two years after Bat Day), that I found in the archives of a now-defunct newspaper called the *New York Reflector*. The article described the circumstances that led to both of the Labrows being in Yankee Stadium that day, and was accompanied by a photo of the couple; in it, Mary and Lyman are smiling and wearing clothes which were already out-of-fashion in 1921. The Grand Canyon is visible in the background. Lyman Labrow was an optometrist and Mary Labrow was a seamstress. They lived in Bergen County, New Jersey, and had no children.

On August 7, 1921, Mary Labrow was sitting one row ahead of me in Yankee Stadium. She was a small, birdlike woman and was wearing a nondescript brown dress that day. She did not look at the field once during the game. Instead, she was looking at two people sitting three rows ahead of her, at a man and a woman.

The man she was looking at was her husband, Lyman Labrow. Mary had come to the game specifically to spy on him, and she could see him perfectly from where she was sitting. Lyman, however, did not see her until it was too late; until she had noticed the same thing I had noticed, that he was not alone.

Lyman Labrow had come to the game that day with his secretary, a twenty-three-year-old woman named Jackie Hubbs. She was wearing a bright yellow dress and carried a small white purse that had a medium-sized bulge in it. She was exactly the kind of girl you look at during baseball games when there is no one at bat.

For the first three innings, no one could have guessed that Lyman Labrow and Jackie Hubbs were romantically involved, despite the fact they were sitting next to one another. They watched the game and their hands did not even touch. Jackie Hubbs' white purse sat chastely on her lap and her white fingers were folded chastely on top of it. However, it became evident during the fourth inning, when Jackie Hubbs reached into her purse and removed the medium-sized bulge, that she and Lyman Labrow were having an affair.

I suppose that today, she and Lyman Labrow could have complicated sexual intercourse in the stands behind third base, and no one would think, or say, anything. But those were different times. On August 7, 1921, Jackie Hubbs caused a sensation in Yankee Stadium by eating a medium-sized Granny Smith apple.

She shined the apple by rubbing it extensively and energetically against her bright yellow dress. Instead of biting into it, she licked it three times, extraordinarily slowly, and handed it to Lyman Labrow. He looked at the apple, took a bite, and gave it back to her. Jackie Hubbs stroked the white part of the apple with her finger, and then touched Lyman Labrow's lips, softly.

And Mary Labrow sat perfectly still, three rows behind them, watching.

Those are the first three people who matter in this story.

The fourth person who matters in this story is a drunken off-duty policeman from Evansville, Indiana, named John Seidl, and the fifth person who matters in this story is a sober Yiddish typewriter salesman from New York City named Norman Flax. John Seidl was sitting in the seat to my right and Norman Flax was sitting directly in front of me.

I know that Norman Flax was a Yiddish typewriter salesman from New York City because he stood up in the bottom of the second inning and introduced himself to a rabbi who was sitting behind me. Norman's mother was sitting beside him, and it was she who pointed out the rabbi to her son. Clearly, Norman Flax was the sort of salesman who was always on the lookout for rabbis.

"I'm Norman Flax," he said, reaching over my head to shake the rabbi's hand. "If you need a Yiddish typewriter, you know who to call."

"I've already got a typewriter," said the rabbi. "What should I need another one for?"

"Maybe you don't need one now," said Norman Flax. "But you never know. When you do need one, call this number and ask for Flax."

And I know that John Seidl was a drunken off-duty policeman from Evansville, Indiana, because he spent most of the game talking loudly to another drunken off-duty policeman from Evansville, Indiana, whose name I never found out.

"I gotta take a leak," announced John Seidl, in the bottom of the fourth inning (just as Jackie Hubbs was reaching for the medium-sized bulge from her purse). "And when John Seidl has to take a leak, John Seidl has to take a leak."

John Seidl was the sort of man who habitually refers to himself in the third person, and that is why I happen to know his name.

"Whattya want me to do?" asked the other off-duty policeman from Evansville, Indiana.

"Ahh," replied John Seidl, as he was standing up. "You're hilarious."

Now: John Seidl was a big man, and when he stood up to make his way out into the aisle, he steadied himself by putting his hand on the shoulder of the person sitting next to him, and almost fell down. It was not a shoulder that provided much support, because it was the shoulder of a ten-year-old boy.

It was my shoulder. That was me. I was sitting beside the sixth person who matters in this story.

Unlike the majority of people in the stands behind third base that day, the sixth person who matters in this story was concentrating on the game. His real name was Giovanni Spadafina, but everyone – even my mother – called him Sampson Spadafina. He was my father.

My father worked at the Heinzman Piano Factory where he was one of twenty-three men responsible for the manufacture of the tiny hammers that strike the strings inside Heinzman pianos. He had come to New York from Italy in 1911 with my mother. "The name of the ship," he used to tell me, "was the *Santa Maria*."

This was something that he said repeatedly. Like Christopher Columbus, my father was from Genoa, and the fact that he landed at Ellis Island in a ship called the *Santa Maria* was of great symbolic importance to him. It allowed him to claim, only half-ironically, that he had arrived in the New World in the same vessel as Columbus. I am aware this is an extremely dubious, if not dangerous, claim to make in this age of political correctness, but it is one that my father – were he still alive today – would continue to make. To my father, Columbus represented everything a man should be: he was intelligent, resourceful, brave, industrious, physically strong, self-sufficient, and very, very rich.

"The Italians," my father used to say, "civilized the world."

When he was not working at the Heinzman Piano Factory he supplemented his income by gambling, and won almost every bet he ever placed. This was not because my father was particularly lucky, but because he always bet on the same thing: himself. He had developed a routine that would usually result in someone agreeing to bet against him. First, he would walk into a bar and order a drink. Then he would begin to talk. He always said the same thing.

"In the Old Country," he would say, "everyone was afraid of me."

Then he would tell the story of his impossible strength, about the earthquake that shook Italy in the spring of 1887, and how the roof of his parents' house landed on his father's legs. He was only a child then, and said he didn't give much thought to what he'd done until after he'd done it. He just lifted the roof off his father.

"And that," he would say, "was when they started calling me Sampson."

The routine usually worked. After he finished telling the story of his impossible strength, the other men in the bar would begin to look at him, to size him up.

The truth is that my father was not a physically imposing man. He was less than five feet tall and did not look strong. There was almost always someone willing to wager he wasn't strong at all.

There were a number of stunts he could perform to demonstrate his impossible strength, and these stunts were usually the subject of the bets he would place. He could pick up tables with his teeth, perform one-arm chin-ups with another man clinging to his back, arm-wrestle three people at once, rip telephone books in half, and on one occasion, I saw him juggle a rusted cannonball, a butcher's knife, and a small St. Bernard.

But my father had to be careful never to go into the same bar too many times. Otherwise people would challenge him to do something that was really impossible. This was what almost happened when he won the tickets to the Yankees game.

I was with him that day. My mother had sent us down to West 88th Street, to the Columbus Bakery, to buy a loaf of bread. On the way he stopped into a bar called O'Malley's and ordered a drink. Then he began to talk.

"In the Old Country," he said, "everybody was afraid of me..."

I suppose that if he had been paying closer attention, he would have seen the look on the bartender's face, how he whispered to another man behind the bar, and the way they both laughed. My father would have known it was a set-up.

"All right, Sampson," said the bartender, "I've got a pair of Yankee tickets right here that say you can't lift the man sitting at the back of the bar."

"That's all?" he asked.

"That's all," said the bartender. "You just lift him up, and you walk out of here with the tickets. If not, then you pay me for the tickets and I keep them."

"*Adesso*," said my father, waving both his hands. In Genoese dialect this is an expression that can mean almost anything. It can be a confirmation, a contradiction, a compliment, a protest, a warning, a congratulation, a shout of dismay, or a way of asking someone to pass the pasta. In that particular context, it was the Genoese equivalent of my father announcing that he was ready to demonstrate his impossible strength.

Everyone followed the bartender to the back of the bar.

It was impossible not to recognize the man my father was required to lift. He was perhaps the most easily identifiable person in the whole of New York. He had been interviewed by every major newspaper, been photographed by the *Guinness Book of World Records*, and had shaken Charlie Chaplin's hand. People came from all over the world to catch a glimpse of him, or to have their photograph taken while sitting on his lap. However, many people declined such a photo opportunity because the man charged a nickel (which in those days was a lot of money) for the privilege. He had a concession at the foot of the Statue of Liberty and it was rumoured that he made a pretty fair living. His real name was Brian Flanagan, but everyone called him what the papers called him: The Fattest Man in New York City.

He was sitting at the back of the bar in a reinforced steel chair, which had been specially constructed to bear his weight. He looked like he had been born in that chair.

When my father saw The Fattest Man in New York City he looked worried. He wiped his hands on his pants. This meant that his palms were sweating. I knew this was a bad sign. My father had palms that never sweated.

"I've made a bet," he whispered to me. "I have to try."

"Good luck," said The Fattest Man in New York City, as my father moved closer to him. "You'll need it."

The bar became completely silent. All I could hear was the sound of my father breathing and The Fattest Man in New York City's uneven wheeze.

"I'm very fat," said The Fattest Man in New York City. "No one has ever lifted me."

"Perhaps I will be the first," said my father, moving to the man.

Now: I knew exactly what my father was thinking. He was thinking about Columbus; about being first. I remember watching my father as he paced circles around The Fattest Man in New York City and – for the first time in my life – wondering if there was something he couldn't do.

I'm not sure exactly how it happened.

"*Adesso*," called out my father, and in a split second, with one perfectly fluid clean-and-jerk movement, it was over. He had somehow taken hold of a foot and a shoulder, and lifted the huge man over his head. The Fattest Man in New York City looked worriedly at the floor, and vomited.

My father quickly put him down, picked up the Yankee tickets and walked out of the bar, wiping off one of his coat sleeves. "Don't tell your mother about this," he said, when we were out on the street, "and I'll take you to the game tomorrow."

They were good seats, but they weren't great seats. My father didn't seem to mind. That was before television, and he had never seen a baseball game before. He had no idea what was going on.

"I understand the strikes," he said to me, "but what's a ball?"

I was about to explain when Babe Ruth came up to bat.

He is the seventh person who matters in this story.

Now: in the bottom of the ninth inning, only the core of Jackie Hubbs' Granny Smith apple remained. She held it between her lips and made a loud sucking noise that drew the attention of everyone sitting in the stands behind third base. I think even Lyman Labrow was embarrassed, although he didn't look like he was about to complain. Mary Labrow found that she could not contain herself any longer. She stood up and spoke to her husband.

This is what she said: "Lyman, you snake, I'm going to kill you."

Unlike myself, John Seidl and the other drunken off-duty policeman from Evansville, Indiana, were paying no attention to the domestic dispute occurring two rows ahead of them. They were deep in conversation. They had already discussed criminals, the criminal mind, specific criminals John Seidl had arrested, the difference between criminals in New York City and criminals in Evansville, the trouble with John Seidl's kids, the trouble with all kids, the trouble with John Seidl's wife, the trouble with having a wife at all, and then, finally, in the bottom of the ninth inning, they began to discuss the 1919 World Series, and who was responsible for fixing it.

"It's them Jews that done it," said John Seidl, loudly.

"I don't know," said the other drunken off-duty policeman from Evansville, Indiana.

"John Seidl is here to tell ya," said John Seidl. "It's them Jews."

"Ain't none of the players that were Jews," pointed out the other man.

Norman Flax turned around in his seat to see who was speaking, and then went back to watching the game.

John Seidl saw him turn around and kept talking.

"It don't matter that none of them was Jews," he said, sounding so ugly that even Norman Flax's mother turned to look at him.

"It was them Jews – they're the ones with the money."

That was when Norman Flax stood up.

"Which Jews exactly?" asked Norman Flax. "Just tell me which of them Jews it was, so that I can get them."

"Siddown, boy," said John Seidl. "You don't want no trouble from John Seidl."

"I'll sit down," said Norman Flax, "when you shut up."

That was when John Seidl stood up.

Babe Ruth stepped into the batter's box. The pitcher threw the first pitch. Babe Ruth took a swing, and hit a high foul ball into the stands behind third base, right where we were sitting.

If it had been any other day at Yankee Stadium nothing would have happened. It would have been a foul ball and the game would have continued.

But it was August 7, 1921.

Bat Day.

Everyone swung at exactly the same time.

Mary Labrow reached across two rows of seats and attempted to hit Lyman Labrow with her complimentary bat. Lyman saw the complimentary bat coming at him and ducked out of the way. In fact, everyone sitting in that row ducked out of the way, with the conspicuous exception of Jackie Hubbs, who, with both of her eyes closed, was preoccupied with sucking an apple core.

The complimentary bat hit her in the face, and flattened her nose completely. There was a strangely silent moment just before Jackie Hubbs began to scream, when she reached up to her nose, and found it crushed.

And Norman Flax reached for his complimentary bat and took a swing at John Seidl.

And John Seidl reached for his complimentary bat and took a swing at Norman Flax.

And both men were knocked instantaneously unconscious. They fell forward and rolled out into the aisle, in each other's arms.

And my father moved with the same unreal fluidity with which he had lifted The Fattest Man in New York City over his head. The foul ball headed right toward us, and before I knew what was happening, he had reached for his complimentary bat and jumped onto his seat.

"*Adesso*," he told me, and bent his knees slightly, and took a swing at the foul ball, and hit it right back at Babe Ruth.

The last thing I remember seeing as we walked quickly out of Yankee Stadium was Babe Ruth lying over home plate. No one knew what had happened. One moment Babe Ruth was hitting his cleats with his bat, and the next, he had collapsed into the dust.

We walked straight home and my father did not say a word. It was not until we got to our house, until he had opened the front door, that he noticed the bat was still in his hands.

"Carmella," he said to my mother, "I think I killed Babe Ruth."

What happened next happened very quickly.

My mother decided that we had to do something. So, we neither waited for the papers the next day (which said that Babe Ruth was still alive), nor went to the police station (which was already filling with the casualties of Bat Day). Instead: we panicked. We packed our things and got on a train the next morning. We came to Canada.

After that, my father stopped doing impossible things. He became a quiet, ordinary carpenter who earned his living building porches and installing kitchen cabinets. People no longer called him Sampson and he never told anyone about August 7, 1921. He died when he was sixty-two years old, of prostate cancer. They sent him home after the treatment had failed. His hair had fallen out and he was completely blind.

The last picture of him was taken just before he died, at my daughter's fifth birthday party. He had already been sent home by the hospital. In the picture he is singing "Happy Birthday," but looking the wrong way as my daughter blows out the candles on her cake. On the table in front of him there are some walnuts that he had cracked open. The nuts are still in them. My father never liked eating walnuts, but loved cracking them open. He would pick up a nut and squeeze it until the shell cracked. He was the only one I ever knew who could do that with only one hand. I've tried it more times than I can count. I suppose that this is the picture that would have to go at the end of his story. Or maybe just a close-up of the walnuts.

August 7, 1921, was the first and last Bat Day in the history of baseball. One hundred eighty-seven people, including Babe Ruth, were injured that day. According to the article in the *New York Reflector*, the Labrows divorced and Jackie Hubbs had reconstructive surgery on her face. In the paper she was quoted as saying that she liked her new nose "better." I have no idea what happened to John Seidl and Norman Flax. The last time I saw them, they were lying with their eyes closed, in each other's arms at the end of our aisle. We stepped over them as we exited the stadium. Perhaps they lived happily ever after.

I still have the complimentary bat that my father got that day. Today it is a rotted piece of wood, and the Yankees logo on its side has faded during the years it was kept in the damp base-ment of my house. The truth is that if I could show it to you, you would be unimpressed. It does not look at all like a bat that might have changed the course of history.

But I still have it. I am an old man now, with grandchildren of my own, but there are days when I go into the basement just to touch it. The feel of the wood never fails to bring back that day, the day my father became afraid. I close my eyes and I can see myself standing beside him in Yankee Stadium. The game is about to begin and both of us are singing "The Star Spangled Banner." His real name was Giovanni, but everyone – even my mother – called him Sampson. I smell the grass and hear the roar of the crowd, the final note dissolving into sunshine.

UMBRELLA

They let you watch television in jail. I don't know why, but I always imagined there would be no television. I suppose that before I got sent here I never gave it much thought. I thought jail was the sort of thing that happened to other people. People on television. But it's not like that at all. It can happen to anyone, like waking up in the morning with a cold, or cancer. We have a television set right in our cell. It's bolted to the wall, underneath the window.

There is no antenna on the set. Instead, a thick black cord comes out of the floor and is welded into the back of the television like a cable connection. But there's no remote control, or dial, or volume knob on the set. It comes on whether we want it to or not. We only get one channel. It's the prison authorities who decide what we get to see. Three years ago we all signed a piece of paper saying it was all right with us for them to put the televisions into our cells. It's part of an experiment in prison reform, aimed at awakening the aesthetic sensibilities of inmates. It's supposed to make us more childlike. Three years ago I remember saying this: "It's just a television, what can they do with that?" Almost everyone signed the paper.

They never let us watch anything sexual or violent. They frequently show us plays by Shakespeare, but only the comedies. I've seen *Twelfth Night* seventeen times since the experiment began. Sometimes they let us watch a hockey game, but not often. Mostly, they make us watch cartoons. In the past three years, I've watched enough cartoons to last me a lifetime. I guess that's the idea.

The cartoons we see most are the ones featuring Sylvester the Cat and Tweety Bird. Sylvester is a black and white clumsy cat with a terrible lateral lisp on the letter S, and Tweety is a resourceful yellow bird with a terrible frontal lisp on the letter T. Each episode begins and ends predictably. It begins with Tweety innocently enjoying life inside his cage somewhere, and during each episode Tweety's safety is seriously threatened by the appearance of Sylvester, who attempts to capture and eat the little bird. However, through his resourcefulness, Tweety always manages to escape. Sylvester is punished – usually brutally – at the end of each episode. They have a complicated, sexy relationship.

"Get that fucking bird" is what Dale Scott yells at the television set each time we watch a Sylvester and Tweety cartoon. He is the other man in my cell. He was formerly a professor of Sociology at the University of Toronto and knows a lot of statistics. Twelve years ago he was sentenced to one hundred and sixty-five years in prison for making movies. In the movies, he would have sex with a woman, usually a student of his – and then suffocate her. He says that he always killed the women in exactly the same way. He would put a transparent plastic bag around her head and wait for the air to run out. He did this for artistic reasons: so that he could film the expression on his victim's face more clearly. According to Dale Scott, only 22.4% of his victims looked surprised when they died.

He is not an easy man to live with. There are deep scars on both of his hands where the women scratched him while trying to pry away his fingers. He has shown them to me several times. You can't help but talk about what you did to get in here, but there are some guys who brag about their crimes. Dale Scott is one of those guys.

He is more critical of the Sylvester and Tweety Bird cartoons than I am. This is what he says about them: "It's so unrealistic – in real life Tweety would never have a chance, Sylvester would catch him 100% of the time."

"But it's just a cartoon," I tell him.

"Exactly," he says. "That's exactly what I'm saying."

My own favourite episode of the Sylvester and Tweety Bird saga involves Sylvester falling off the top of an apartment building. It happens right at the end of the episode, after Sylvester has failed – once again – to capture Tweety Bird. For some reason, Sylvester is holding an umbrella when he falls off the building. During his descent, Sylvester looks right out of the television and shrugs his shoulders. He opens the umbrella, smiles, and waves. Then he hits the pavement.

I think the way Sylvester opens the umbrella says a lot about him. It shows he is a very self-aware cat. He knows he will never get to eat Tweety Bird. He knows that he will always be falling off tall buildings. But still he opens the umbrella. It is the only dignity available to him. It is the obscure elegance of a cat about to hit the pavement.

While I am watching television I sometimes try to write about why I'm here. Dale Scott has read most of what I've written. He says that 98.8% of all criminals feel the urge to confess at one time or another, and that he would be worried if I did not feel like it. I point out to him that he does not seem to share this impulse to write.

"Sure I do," he tells me. "But I tell people, I never write anything down – you can never know whether it'll be used as part of your offence or part of your defence."

This is Dale Scott's criminal philosophy. It is uniquely Canadian, and is perhaps the only thing he's ever said that makes sense to me.

Dale Scott says crime is like a hockey game. You commit an offence and then you have to play defence.

"You're crazy," he tells me. "They'll get hold of this and then you'll never get out of here."

He's probably right, but I know I have to write it down. I know that I wouldn't be able to survive in here if I didn't write something down. I know what I have to do. Like Sylvester, I'm a very self-aware cat.

This is the story.

It begins with me standing in a butcher's shop with a hockey stick in my hands.

I am looking out the big glass window at the front of the shop. On the window, the words EVANS MEATS are written in large red capital letters. It is 3:45 pm. There are people walking by on the sidewalk but there are no customers inside the shop. I don't look directly at any of the people walking by, but I can see them, and I know most of their names. Ballentine Hill is the town in which this story takes place. It is one of those towns where everybody knows everybody else.

It is not a busy street but it is one of the main streets in the town. There was a time when my father thought himself lucky to secure such a prime location for his butcher shop. It's right near the centre of town. Down the street from the police station. Next door to the post office. Behind the IGA. Right across from the optometrist's office.

I am holding a hockey stick with both of my hands and pressing the butt of it against my front teeth. I am gripping it so tightly that the knuckles on both of my hands have turned white. I am doing this because the perfect moment of my life occurred when I was playing hockey.

I was eighteen years old and playing right wing for the Ballentine Hill Raiders. Someone passed me the puck when I was standing in front of the other team's net. The name of the other team was the Brampton Wolverines. I got control of the puck by stickhandling quickly and turned around to face the goalie.

Then I smiled.

I smiled because I knew what was going to happen next.

I put the puck into the upper right hand corner of the net. It was the only goal of the game. Everybody in the arena went wild. When the buzzer sounded to signal the end of the first period, we were winning one to nothing. The coach took me aside in the dressing room and told me there was a scout from the Toronto Maple Leafs sitting in the stands, and that he wanted to talk to me after the game was over.

Since then, the feel of the hockey stick in my hands never fails to bring back that moment to me. The feel of the goal. The calm of knowing what is going to happen next.

Even now I wish I could touch a hockey stick. But they won't let me have one in the cell. I suppose they are afraid I will use it as a weapon. I can't argue with that.

I used to keep the stick in the butcher's shop. Before I was in jail there were certain days when I would go in there just to touch it. These were days when I thought I couldn't cope. Dale Scott says that 95.6% of all people have those kinds of days on a regular basis. I am no exception.

This story begins on one of those days. The stick is in my hands, but I am not remembering how I scored that goal. Instead, I am thinking about Celia. About what I am going to say. I am telling myself to just walk in there and tell her what I think of her, and I am imagining what the look on her face will be like.

Celia is my wife. I was introduced to her by my mother. This is how it happened: we were in IGA and my mother started talking to the cashier. Celia was the cashier. They knew each other well enough to say hello. My mother shopped at IGA most of the time.

"This is my son, Malcolm," said my mother.

"Pleased to meet you," said Celia, shaking my hand.

I knew right away she recognized me. I could tell she was trying not to stare, that she was trying not to look at my teeth. After I carried my mother's groceries out to the car I went back into the supermarket and asked Celia if she wanted to go to a movie with me that Friday.

And that was the way our romance began. Like the rest of Ballentine Hill, Celia was a bit scared of me at first. She was afraid because of what happened to me in the second period of that game against the Brampton Wolverines.

It was the last hockey game I ever played. I was injured near the beginning of the second period. A defenceman from my own team took a slap shot from the blue line just as I lost my footing. The puck did more than knock out thirteen teeth. It lodged itself lengthwise in my mouth and needed to be surgically removed in the hospital.

"I've never seen anything like it," said the coach, as he knelt beside me on the ice. Then he stood up and waved to the bench for someone to bring out a stretcher.

"That puck is right the fuck in there," said Frank Fitzhenry. I remember that he looked guilty when he said that. He was the defenceman who had taken the shot. He looked at his stick like it had nothing to do with him.

I don't know what happened next. They gave me a shot of something and I felt like I was floating out of the arena. It took a while to get to the ambulance because of the photographer. A photo of my shattered mouth appeared on the front page of the Ballentine Hill Herald the next day. My mother didn't show me the paper until I was out of the hospital.

When I was discharged from the hospital I went back and tried to play hockey. But it was somehow different. Even I knew it. The coach told me to take my time, but soon everyone figured out that my problem didn't have anything to do with my teeth. I would stand in the corner of the rink and hope that no one passed me the puck. I thought constantly about untying my skates. That was when I stopped playing hockey.

I graduated from high school and went to work with my father at EVANS MEATS. I did my own thing. I worked during the day and watched television with my parents in the evening. On Friday and Saturday nights I would go out with my high-school buddies and get drunk. But then I met Celia and I felt my life was ready to change.

We got married on July 10, 1982. I rented a huge white limousine and we drove around town after the wedding. People came out of their houses and waved to us as we passed by. Everyone knew who I was. It was a beautiful day, with hardly a cloud in the sky.

But when this story begins, my wedding day is more than ten years old. I am standing in the butcher's shop with a hockey stick in my hand and looking across the street. At the optometrist's office.

This is because I have just found out that my wife is fucking the optometrist.

At the trial Celia insisted that the affair began innocently. I never knew anything about it. She said that it started, really, on the afternoon when she burned her eyelashes.

She was getting ready to fry some potatoes when the telephone rang. She says that she talked on the phone for less than a minute, and then went back to the stove. When she dropped the first potato into the pan, it burst into flames. She grabbed it and threw it into the sink. When I came home that night, she said she was shaken up, but not hurt.

The next day her left eye started to bother her. She told me it felt like someone was sticking a hundred little needles into it. I took her to the optometrist.

"You've got entropion of your left eye," said Dr. Patrick Morgan. "Have you been in some kind of fire?"

Celia told him about the frying pan.

"That'll do it," he said, and explained that entropion meant her eyelashes had been burned. They were curled inwards, and were slightly touching her eyeball. These were the little needles she had been feeling. "It's not a big problem," he told her. "But you'll have to come in once a week to get your eyelashes plucked."

I don't have all the details, but at the trial Celia confessed that the affair began during her third appointment. She told the jury that Dr. Patrick Morgan was plucking out her eyelashes and realized, with some embarrassment, that his hand was resting on the inside of her thigh. She didn't stop him. That was exactly the way she said it: "I didn't stop him."

They established a routine.

Dr. Patrick Morgan would tell his receptionist to call Celia and schedule an appointment. Even if she were at home when the receptionist called, Celia would let the answering machine take the call. She would purposefully forget to erase the message, and always made sure I heard it.

"My eyelashes are growing at a phenomenal rate," she told me once.

And on the day this story begins (but before it actually begins), I found out about the affair.

It was three o'clock in the afternoon when I walked across the street to the optometrist's office. There were no customers in the butcher's shop and I put a sign in the window saying that I would be back in an hour. I'd been having trouble seeing the television clearly for some time and, earlier that day, I'd imagined that I'd seen a woman who looked very much like my wife visit the optometrist's office twice. So: I decided to get my eyes checked. I didn't call ahead for an appointment. I just walked across the street.

I was surprised to find the office completely empty. Not even the receptionist was there. The door to the examination room was closed and the only sound in the room was coming from behind it.

I sat down in one of the chairs in the waiting room and pretended to be reading a magazine. I waited for five minutes. I could hear something was going on behind the closed door, but couldn't make out what either person was saying. I decided to come back at another time. I stood up and started to walk out of the office.

That was when I heard his voice. "Celiahhhhhhh!" called out Dr. Patrick Morgan, suddenly.

I turned around and walked toward the door of the examination room. I turned the knob very gently and looked inside. I couldn't believe what I saw.

Dr. Patrick Morgan was completely naked. His hands were handcuffed behind his back. His feet were tied down with thick ropes to the bottom of the examination chair. He had a massive erection.

My wife was pulling out his chest hairs, individually.

Each time she yanked out a hair he would moan. Then Celia slapped him across the face several times. She told him that he deserved whatever he got from her. He seemed to agree. She was naked except for a pair of leather underwear. I watched for about a minute. Then I closed the door gently. I walked out of the office and back across the street. I stood behind the counter of the butcher's shop and took the hockey stick into my hands.

And that is when this story begins.

I am looking out the big glass window at the front of the shop. It is 3:45 pm. I have been standing there for half an hour, thinking about what I am going to say to Celia. I am gripping the stick so tightly that the knuckles on both of my hands have turned white.

I do not know exactly when I begin to walk across the street. There is still no one in the optometrist's office when I open the examination room door for the second time.

My wife is sitting in the examination chair.

Dr. Patrick Morgan has a pair of forceps in his right hand, and he is holding Celia's eye open with the other. They both have their clothes on, and he has just said something that made her laugh. He is plucking her eyelashes. They both turn around when I open the door. Dr. Patrick Morgan is wearing a metal headband with a light attached to the front of it, and when he turns around it shines into my eyes.

"I know," I say. "I know about you both."

"Know about what?" asks Celia.

"Don't fuck with me," I tell her.

"Just take it easy," says Dr. Patrick Morgan. "What's the problem?"

"What's the problem?" I reply. "I'll tell you what the problem is."

It is then that I realize I have nothing to say. It is like the whole thing is happening to someone else. Someone on television. I am thinking exactly that when I realize the hockey stick is still in my hands. And that is the second time in my life that I know exactly what is going to happen next.

When it is over, I walk quietly out of the office.

I can hear Celia screaming and I feel very tired as I unlock the door to the butcher's shop. The blood of Dr. Patrick Morgan blends inconspicuously into the front of my butcher's apron, only slightly fresher than the other blood on it. The stick is still in my hands. The police arrive across the street in less than a minute. We are right near the centre of town, and the police station is just down the street. There was probably a time when Dr. Patrick Morgan thought himself lucky to secure such a prime location for his office.

The policemen run into his office, and a couple of minutes later they come toward the butcher shop. They put me into the back of the squad car and take me to the police station. They send me here. They put me in a cell with Dale Scott and make me watch cartoons.

And that is the end of the story.

Dale Scott says he approves, on the whole, of what I've written. He is impressed that I haven't tried to prove my innocence. He tells me that he has just read an article about an experiment done in a prison in British Columbia, in which inmates were told to write an essay about their crimes. He says that 94.9% of those who participated tried to justify their actions. I am part of that missing 5.1%. I think that makes him nervous.

However, Dale Scott is also critical of this story. He says that it lacks closure, that too much is left hanging.

"Look at *Twelfth Night*," he tells me. "Now that's a story with closure – at the end of it everyone is married and lives happily ever after. When it's over, you really feel like it's over."

"But what about Malvolio?" I ask him. "He doesn't marry anyone."

"Malvolio is different," he replies. "He gets what he deserves."

I have only seen Celia once since the trial. I like to think that she would come to see me more often if she wasn't in the hospital. Her sickness is not life threatening, but the doctors have no idea how to cure it. Dale Scott says that it is an extremely rare kind of mental disorder, although he admits that he doesn't know, exactly, how rare it is.

Celia's problem is that she can't stand to see other people move their hands when they talk. She will be speaking to someone and then, quite suddenly, she will feel a compulsion to grab hold of their hands. She was sent to the hospital after she broke a bank teller's ring finger. It was an accident. Celia says she never meant to hurt the woman, and I believe her. She says she just wanted to keep the woman's hands still. I talk to Celia once a week on the telephone. She says some days are better than others.

The last time I saw her was just after the trial, before she got sick. We sat across from each other in the visitors room and tried to think of something to say.

"Yesterday," I remember telling her, "we got a television in our cell."

"That's good," she replied. "You always did like television."

And then we were silent again. We sat like that for fifteen minutes, and I know now that Celia was trying not to look at my hands, that she was trying very hard to sit still. Finally, she got up to leave.

"I'm sorry about all this," I told her. "This wasn't supposed to happen to us."

She looked at me. "I know that," she said.

Just before she left, she wiped away a tear from her left eye and I noticed that the eyelashes that Dr. Patrick Morgan had been plucking out that day had grown back. They were as long and as dark as they had ever been. Celia turned around and walked out of the visitors room without saying anything else. It was the last time I saw her.

And that really is the end of this story. From this cell, life looks less like Shakespeare and more like a Sylvester and Tweety Bird cartoon. There is always someone in a cage. There is always someone required to fall off the ledge of a tall building. There is always someone just about to hit the pavement. This story is the opening of my umbrella.

STARK COUNTY
BASEBALL

Right from the start, I didn't want to do the reading at the Stark
Public Library in Stark County, Ohio, which, as anyone from
there will tell you, is a straight shot down Route 77 from
Cleveland where I live. It's a quick hour. This is the kind of thing
they say in Stark County, Ohio with about the same frequency as
they say, in other parts of the world, that it looks like rain.

I was promised that if I got there early I'd get a tour of the
Football Hall of Fame, which is the jewel of Canton, Ohio, smack
dab in the center of Stark County. It was Wendell Horn, President of the Friends of the Stark County Public Library, who made
this offer when he called to ask me to come to read. The other
thing he said was that he had heard that I was a lot of fun. This
was something that another writer had said about me, apparently, when she'd been down in Stark County to read herself.

"A lot of fun," said Wendell Horn on the phone. "That was all
I needed to hear."

I told him I'd be there for the reading. "All the same," I said,
"I think I'll skip the tour of the Football Hall of Fame."

"I see," said Wendell.

"I mean, if it's OK by you."

"No problem."

Then he told me that, instead of inside the Stark County
Public Library, I would be giving my reading outside – at the Stark
County Ballpark.

"Don't you worry," he told me. "We're wired."

"That's good," I said.

"I mean for sound," he said.

"You know what?" I said. "Why don't we just have it in the library?"

When I said this, Wendell Horn just laughed.

By the time it was time for the reading, the snow was gone. It was springtime in Ohio, which, next to the fall, is the best time of year here. As I drove the straight shot along Route 77 on my way out of Cleveland, I allowed myself to think that it wasn't going to be that bad. I've discovered this is the kind of thing you say to yourself when you're a writer, when you're on the way to a reading. I read somewhere about Balzac giving a reading atop a large block of cheddar cheese, and that Morde-cai Richler had telecast a whole series of CBC interviews from inside a Remy Martin bottle. Hell, if Richler could allow him-self to be locked into a glass prison, who was I to complain about driving out to Stark County or reading outside? It was a straight shot from Cleveland, after all. There were versions of the story about Richler in which it was Richler's idea to read from inside the liquor bottle. If they wanted me to read at a baseball park, I told myself, I'd read at a goddamn baseball park. I'd stand on the mound, for all I cared, and belt it out into the stands. If they wanted me to chew tobacco, I'd chew it. Then I'd get my cheque and I'd get the hell out of there. As I drove, I tried my best to manufacture what I believed would have been Richler's attitude toward the whole thing which was, more or less, to know the whole thing was ridiculous, and to do it anyway.

The baseball park was about a mile and a half off the high-way, just east of Stark Tires, across the street from a wrecked and dilapidated movie theatre. Wendell Horn was there waiting for me just inside the entrance to the stadium, standing exactly where he promised he would.

"I'm Steven Hayward," I told him.

"It's a real pleasure, Dr. Hayward," he said. The way he said doctor had a bit of a sneer in it. It reminded me of the way my mother said it, out of the corner of her mouth, as if to say it wouldn't be the worst thing in the world if one of her kids turned out to be a real doctor instead of having a so-called doctorate in English Literature. "Any trouble getting here?"

"None at all," I told him.

"So the map worked?"

"The map was excellent," I said, and then with that giddiness that sometimes descends upon a literary unknown like myself when he finds himself a guest of honour, I heard myself adding, a moment later, "It was one of the best maps I've seen."

It was, I see now, too much. Whatever else can be said about him, Wendell Horn was no fool; he was a tall man with white, elaborately trimmed eyebrows, and he knew when he was being condescended to. It startled him. Though Canton is just an hour south of Cleveland, there's a distinct twang in people's accents that's unheard in the bigger city, which is a reminder that you aren't far from West Virginia and Kentucky. There is also a kind of Southern gentility down there, a time-worn conviction that civility is a cardinal virtue. Though I tried to make light of it, tried, as it were, to retract the comment, it was too late. Wendell had already changed his mind about me. I suppose I know for a fact that what happened next didn't only happen because of that single moment of ill-considered sarcasm, and that the Stark County Library didn't change their plans just because they found themselves confronted by an ironic Canadian like myself, but it didn't help. Whatever the case may be, it was at that moment I noticed Wendell Horn was wearing a baseball uniform. Before I could comment on it, though, he took a step backwards, looked at me and shook his head, and this is what he said: "You're not going to pitch in that."

I was dressed the way authors are supposed to dress: in black jeans, a black T-shirt, black sports coat, and shiny black shoes.

"Pitch?" I said.

Once again, Wendell Horn just laughed.

As if it were a medieval church in a medieval town in the south of France, the baseball diamond behind the Stark County Library was the most splendid thing about Stark County. The lights snapped on as Wendell and I came in through a small door in the right field fence and veritably glinted off the backstop, reflecting toward the sky the immaculate green of the turf, the immaculate blue of the home run fence. Unlike most other ball-parks I had been to in Ohio, where advertisements of all sorts are stuck everywhere it is plausible or possible to do so, the home run fence at the Stark County Ballpark was an unpolluted vista, virgin territory.

"Is this heaven," I said, "or is this Ohio?"

"Ohio," said Wendell Horn.

"That's from *Field of Dreams*," I said. "You know, with Kevin Costner in it."

"I don't know it."

"It's by a Canadian," I told him. "W.P. Kinsella, I mean, the book that came before the movie – actually it was a story first. Anyway, he's a Canadian."

"You know," said Wendell Horn, "I did *not* know that. But I don't know the movie, as I said. I don't care much for movies about the game. I care for the game, if you catch me."

"Actually, Kinsella's from Manitoba," I said. I didn't even know if that was true. I had no idea where he was from. It made sense that he was from somewhere out west, but maybe it was all the way out west. "Yes," I said, rambling, "he's as Canadian as the day is long."

By this time Wendell Horn had stopped listening to me. We were now at the pitcher's mound, where I found myself looking at the whole of the Stark County Library Board, who were sitting on a bench in the dugout, impatiently, like kids waiting to be put into a game.

"Well," said Wendell Horn, then, pressing a baseball into my hand, "Let's see what you're made of, Mr. Baseball Writer."

I realized then that he had left me standing on the mound. "What's going on?"

"What's going on," jeered one of the octogenarians on the bench. He was completely bald, and for some reason speaking in a high falsetto voice.

"I thought I was giving a reading," I said. "From my novel."

"From my novel," echoed the old man again, still in falsetto.

The rest of the old men on the bench laughed their heads off.

"I don't know why you're laughing," I said.

This made them laugh more. Some of them were so old and laughing so hard that I wondered if it might kill them. I should have left then. I should have driven back to Cleveland, picked up my wife and kids and put them into the car and kept driving, all the way north, back to Toronto. But we had a mortgage and one of the kids had a cold and I needed the money. "Listen," I said. "I don't know what is going on here but I don't think it's very funny."

This stopped no one.

"Come on, Mr. Baseball Writer," said Wendell Horn. "Let's see what you're made of."

"Flesh and bone," I said. "Like anyone."

"You wish," shouted a different one of the old guys on the bench.

"You wish," said another one of the guys to the first one.

Then everyone laughed like hell again.

"Let me tell you," said Wendell Horn, swinging the bat over the plate. "Your book isn't bad, for being a book."

"Well," I said, lamely, "it *is* a book."

"Listen," he said. "I'm president of the Stark County Library Board. I can tell a book when I see one."

"I'm leaving," I said.

Wendell Horn seemed to know I was just bluffing. "Maybe you can write," he said, "but you know nothing about baseball."

"It's a work of fiction," I told him.

Wendell Horn hoisted the bat to his shoulder. "Go ahead," he said.

"I'm not going to do this," I said.

"I'm not going to do this," said the old guy with the falsetto voice. Maybe it was his real voice, I found myself thinking, maybe he just talks like that.

"Really," I said. "I mean, I mean it."

"Really," whined the guy on the bench.

"What're you worried about," said Wendell Horn. "I'm an old man."

"I'm an old man," called out the guy on the bench in the falsetto voice. Then, a moment later a deeper voice, "Sorry, Wendell."

"One pitch and I get my cheque and go – deal?"

"Deal," he said.

"I have your word?"

"Shut up and pitch," he told me.

And so I got ready. I took off my jacket, and I stretched a little. I worked my right shoulder and I flexed my fingers. I was taking a long time and I knew it, I could tell that several of the old men on the bench were beginning to fall asleep. One of them got up to relieve himself. And then, in much the same way that a single yawning person is supposed to create the need to yawn in those around him, the rest of the men on the bench got up to relieve themselves. They did this by stepping into the semi-darkness of the field's edge, as if there were no choice about it and there weren't bathrooms somewhere inside the stadium, just a few feet away. I took my time, thinking that Wendell Horn could not be immune, but he was.

"I can wait all night," he told me. "I've had a colostomy."

Seeing there was no choice, I went into my windup. I suppose that in the version of this story they'll tell at my funeral, I will lob a soft underhand pitch toward Wendell Horn, a pitch that anyone, even the guys who have had colostomies, can knock clear over the right field wall. In that version of this story, I will watch the ball sail over my head and smile at the vagaries of human existence with a benign acceptance of it all. Or at least, I will not throw a knuckleball. I will, instead, throw a fastball. Or some approximation of it. A slow fastball that Wendell Horn can knock over the right field fence and I'll go over and shake his hand. He'll hand me a cheque and I'll go back to my normal life as a writer who knows nothing about baseball, really. This story will have a happy ending.

But this is what really happened:

I did throw a knuckleball, which I should not have done because, in the first place, I wanted Wendell Horn to hit the ball, and in the second place, it isn't one of those pitches I have, so to speak, in my arsenal. It was a pitch I had read about. I had taken out books from the library and seen the pictures, and had even tried holding a baseball in my hand in the way I might have if I was going to throw a knuckleball. But I had not thrown one before. It was a theoretical pitch, as far as I was concerned.

I regretted it the moment it left my hand. Though I began to regret it more when I saw that Wendell Horn knew I was going to throw a knuckleball, as if there was someone in the back of the stadium with my stats who had run those numbers through a computer and signalled to Wendell that he should be ready for a knuckleball – and for that reason Wendell Horn stepped forward and got ready to bunt.

And bunt he did, laying it down perfectly on the third base line. It was lovely to see, though if there had been a catcher there is no question that he would have been out at first, for he was an old man with a colostomy bag, the kind of guy who never could run very quickly to begin with and now could hardly run at all. But there was no catcher and I lunged forward, fielded the ball myself and sprinted like hell after Wendell Horn. As slow as he was moving, he was nearly at first base by the time I caught up to him. I'd like to be able to say that I didn't dive to make the out, but I did. I hit the old man with such force that we both fell to the ground just beyond first base.

"Safe," called a voice.

I looked around, not sure who was speaking or where the voice was coming from.

"Safe," said the voice again, and out of the shadows stepped the ghost of Mordecai Richler.

"Holy cow," I said.

"Holy cow?" said the ghost of Mordecai Richler. "I come back from the dead and this is the most you can manage." It was not a question.

"Sorry," I said.

"And now you're apologizing," said the ghost.

"Sorry," I began to say again, then stopped. " I love your work," I said. "I mean, you're such an inspiration."

"Inspiration," snorted Mordecai Richler's ghost. "Let me tell you, it's no picnic."

"Sorry to hear that," I said.

It was then that I noticed that Wendell Horn had got up off the grass. He dusted himself off and, like a true gentleman, walked over and gave me the cheque. "A real pleasure," he said, and made me promise that if I ever found myself in Stark County that I would look him up. A kind of jubilant feeling came over me, and on our way out to the parking lot I asked the ghost of Mordecai Richler if I could buy him a drink. He said he could use one but that he had a long drive ahead of him. Wendell Horn said the same thing. So it was that when we finally got out under the big lights of the parking lot I turned my back for just a moment and everyone else there – Wendell Horn, the ghost of Mordecai Richler, the guy on the bench who had heckled me in the weird falsetto – vanished into thin air. I wasn't surprised. I got into the car and drove back to Cleveland and had a beer in the kitchen with my wife, who wanted to know what had happened. She said I should write it down. And that is what happened, or at least, the kind of thing that *can* happen when you're talking about that old, old game, that ancient thing called baseball.

TO DANCE
THE BEGINNING
OF THE WORLD

I[1] won Columbus the goldfish accidentally at the Richmond Hill
Spring Fair in the summer of 1972. In itself, this may not seem
like such a noteworthy event,[2] but it happened during the great
date of my life.[3] There is nothing that can ruin a date more effec-
tively than a goldfish.[4]

---

[1] Of course, I am no longer the insecure teenager I once was, but I refuse to play the
complicated post-modem games that so many writers love to engage in. This is not a
riddle of delayed signification, it is a pure story; the story of how I lost my virginity.

[2] A goldfish life consists of swimming, eating, and defecating. Nothing remarkable ever
happens. Even the death of a goldfish occurs without much fanfare. You wake up one
morning to discover that the goldfish is not swimming as well as it did the day before.
The next morning you find that it is unable to do anything other than float listlessly at
the top of the bowl. Then suddenly–almost as if it intends to catch you by surprise–it
splashes violently around in the bowl. These are its death throes. And this is the
moment when it is most alive. The fish understands nothing except that it does not
want to die. It dies anyway. When it finally stops moving, you flush it down the toilet.
Human beings treat each other in much the same way. When my wife (now my ex)
called to say she was leaving me, I put the phone down very slowly and cried for the
first time in fifteen years. I felt like the inside of a goldfish bowl.

[3] Of course, now that I can consider my life maturely as a whole, I can see that it was
not the great date of my life, but only one of the great dates of my life. I like to think
that the great date of my life is still ahead of me. I am only thirty-five, and this is something which I need to believe.

[4] With the possible exception of herpes. There is absolutely nothing which ruins a date
more than realizing the other person has herpes. This has never actually happened to
me, but I can imagine what it would be like. The closest I have ever come was in grade
thirteen, when Norma Fullerstein informed me she had mono after we'd kissed.

My name is Brian Canham, and I was once a sixteen-year-old virgin. I remember days when I felt like I was the only person on the planet who had not done it yet.[5] I am now seventeen, and of course, I have done it many times, but I can still remember what it was like never to have done it.

Our school expert on doing it is Peter Campbell. Peter is a tall blond guy who is captain of the basketball team. Peter goes out with Trish, a girl with huge dark eyes. She plays clarinet in the school band and comes to every basketball game.[6] Although she is the best-looking girl in the school, Peter cheats on her all the time. It seems like Peter is always doing it, and that when he is not actually doing it, he is thinking about new ways of doing it, or new people to do it with.

It was Peter who first gave me the idea to ask Diane out. We were warming up for a game when Peter dribbled over to me and pointed out Diane Vitesse in the stands.

"Do you know her?" he asked.

"Sure," I replied. "Why?"

"She thinks you're cute."

---

[5] Every period has its own euphemism for sex: boff, boink, bop, bang, hump, fuck, do the dirty deed, ride the lizard, play hide the sausage, coitus, laying pipe, the old in-out, schtupping, slapping bellies, tonsil hockey, hanging the chandelier, frisking the pony, making the beast with two backs, the hot and sloppy, getting down and dirty, getting it on, getting it, doing it, plugging it – the list goes on and on, but it all means the same thing. In Elizabethan times, they called it, among other things, "to dance the beginning of the world." I think they knew what they were talking about: sex is the beginning and the end of the world; it is why it really counts in the universe. My wife (now my ex) tells me her new lover is a young artist. I don't want to know what he looks like.

[6] However, while she came to all the games, she never came at any of the games. This sort of thing does not happen in high school, or at least didn't at my high school – it was in the suburbs. It was not until I was in university, when I met an Italian girl named Florence Berlini, that I had sex in a public place. We dated for about two months, but broke up because I couldn't take it any more. We would do it everywhere. On elevators, in public washrooms, in movie theatres, in cloakrooms, in closets and on buses. But she would never let me actually sleep with her. Sex in bed was boring, she said. Maria (my ex) used to hate it when I talked about Florence. Sometimes it is hard to remember that we aren't married any more. I still can't sleep on her side of the bed.

"How do you know?"

"Trish told me."

"What did she say?"

"Trish said that the other day when they were in geography and Mr. Conway left the room they each wrote out lists of who they thought were the best-looking guys, and you were number two on her list."

"Really? Who was number one?"

"I was…but that doesn't matter – she would never do it with me."

"Why?"

"Because I'm not the right kind of guy. You are. Diane is just waiting for the right kind of guy to do it with. She hasn't done it yet, but she will.

"So what should I do?"

"Ask her out," he said simply, and dribbled away.

During the game, each time I got a basket, I would look up at Diane in the stands, to see her reaction. Once – after a turn-around jump shot from just behind the foul line – I looked up into the stands, and she waved at me.[7]

Peter was right, she did think I was cute. Tomorrow, before math class, I would ask her out.[8]

---

[7] In high school, a wave is a definite indication of love. Girls in high school don't just wave at anybody. And this was no ordinary wave; it was a wave with weight. It is only in later life, after sour love affairs and selfish people have calloused one's heart, that a wave becomes insignificant. A wave – in high school – is not unlike a phone call late in the night, during which the person on the other end of the line doesn't say a word, but nevertheless communicates, by simply breathing, their name and that they think they cannot live without you.

[8] At the time, it seemed as if everything in my life had been transformed. When the game was over, I ran all the way home and helped my sister set the table. After dinner, I kissed my mother on the cheek and told her that the meal was delicious. My father came up to my room later in the evening and asked me if I was taking drugs. I explained that I was in love. "Don't tell your mother," he said quickly, and closed the door behind him.

The next day, I got to math class early, right after lunch. Diane always arrived a little early for class, so it was no problem knowing where to find her. The math teacher had not yet opened the door, and when I got there she was standing outside the classroom, alone. I knew that if I hesitated I would chicken out, so I just took a deep breath, walked up to her and started talking.[9]

"Hi Diane," I said. "How are you?"

"Fine," she replied.

"Fine," I said, not realizing that she had not asked me, then added, "You're looking nice today."

"Why, thank you," she answered. For a moment we looked at each other in silence. I looked at my shoes, and Diane lightly shook her pencil case.

Then she broke the silence.

"You played a really good game yesterday."

"Thanks."

For a moment we just looked at each other. She scratched behind her ear; I took a deep breath. Then we both laughed.

"Do you want to go out Friday?" I said suddenly.

"Like on a date?"

Holding my breath, I nodded.

She looked away, at the math book in her hands, "I guess."

"Really?" I exclaimed, finally exhaling.

"Sure, why not?" she asked.

"I don't know."

"You don't know what?"

"I don't know why not."

---

[9] Asking her was like jumping into a swimming pool. I felt like I was standing on a diving board and looking into the cold water beneath me. When you dive into a pool there is always that moment – when you are suspended in mid-air when you wonder whatever made you want to get wet in the first place.

"Neither do I," she said.

"So then, it's OK?" I said to be sure.

"It's OK," she said with finality.

Then we both laughed.[10]

"When do you want to meet?" she asked.

"Eight?"

"Sure," she said. "Maybe we could go to the fair."

"Good idea."

I can't recall anything about math class that day other than the discovery that by turning my head in a certain way, I could look at Diane and the math teacher at the same time.

I wondered what it would be like to kiss her. Was I really in love?[11] I wondered what she was thinking. I wondered if she was thinking about me. I started to think about what our date would be like. I would walk over to her house and pick her up around eight.

Then we would take the bus to the fair. We would go on some rides, get something to eat, and then I would walk her home. Then, what would happen? I wondered if she liked me enough to do it. Soon, I was thinking about actually doing it.

That was when I began to get nervous.

Really nervous.

In fact, I started to panic. I considered telling her after school that I couldn't make it that night. I could say that I had

---

[10] It has been said that there is comfort in knowing that you are damned, but there is damn more comfort in knowing that you have a date.

[11] This was a much easier question then – when I had never been in love before – than it is today. At sixteen love seemed like a great adventure. Today, I don't even know what love is. Six months ago, when Maria and I spoke for the last time, I started to cry again. On the phone, she seemed like a different person. I asked what I had done to deserve this.

"It wasn't your fault," she told me. "Stop torturing yourself."

"Then why?" I asked. "Why did it have to happen?"

"People change," she said and hung up the phone.

just remembered a family commitment, or that I had to take my brother to the doctor. I could get someone else to go with her. I could ask Peter. She thought he was cuter than me anyway. I could just not show up. But then she would tell her friends and I would never get a date for the rest of my life. I could call her that night and say that I had come down with the flu, but then I would have to stay at home and my parents would think I was taking drugs. There seemed to be no way out.

When the class ended, I ran out of the classroom as fast as I could, not even looking at Diane. By the time I walked into basketball practice after school I was a nervous wreck.

"What's the matter with you?" asked Peter as we changed into our gym clothes.

"I just asked Diane out," I told him shakily.

"Really," he said. "Where are you going?"

"To the fair."

"Right on!" he said, shaking his fist the same way he does when someone on the team scores a foul shot.

"Hey, everybody," he called out to the change room in general, "Brian has a date with Diane."

"Right on," everyone called back, shaking their fists.

John Pesner, the centre on the team, walked over to me. I thought he was going to shake my hand, but he didn't. Instead, he pressed a little plastic package in my palm.

"Don't forget to put your boots on," he said.

I looked at the white package and smiled weakly.

"You're not shooting blanks anymore," he reminded me as the changeroom suddenly became very quiet.

Putting the condom between my teeth, I bent down to tie my shoes. "Yeah," I said weakly, trying my best to mean it, "I know what I'm doing. She's just waiting for the right guy."

"Right on," said an unfamiliar deep voice. It was Mr. Williams, the basketball coach. He was making the fist.[12]

At the fair, the air smelled of grass cuttings, gasoline, cigarettes and candy floss. Diane was wearing a white dress and high heels. With her heels on, she was about two inches taller than me. She looked very different than at school, where she wore jeans most of the time. I didn't comment on it, however, figuring that she was thinking the same thing about me. I was wearing ripped jeans, a black Van Halen T-shirt, white Reebox shoes, and Aqua Velva aftershave.[13]

"What do you want to do first?" I asked as we walked toward the entrance.

"It's up to you," she said cheerfully, and began to hold my hand.

I didn't want to go on rides yet, and it was too early to get anything to eat, so I suggested that we play some of the games.

"That looks like fun." Diane pointed at a booth where a huge red bear was hanging. Underneath the bear was a multicoloured pyramid of goldfish bowls.

"Let's give it a try," I said.

"What do you do?" I asked the guy who ran the stand.

"It's easy," he told me. "You throw the ball, and if it lands in the bowl filled with red water, you get the bear. If it lands in one of the other bowls, you get another prize. As long as you get it in a bowl, you get a prize. Everyone's a winner."

It really didn't look that difficult. There was only one bowl with red water, and it was at the top. You either got the ball right into it, or missed completely. I got three balls for a dollar.

---

[12] Mr. Williams was so politically incorrect that he was politically uncorrect. Even his grammar was offensive.

[13] I was dressed to kill.

My first try missed the pyramid of bowls completely.[14] I threw the ball straight at the red bowl as hard as I could. I wanted to put it straight in. The ball did not even touch any of the bowls. It was very embarrassing.

I threw the next ball on a wide arch, aiming as closely as possible at the red bowl.[15] But again, I missed all of the bowls.

"Good throw," said Diane, and kissed me softly on the cheek.

"That was for good luck," she told me when I looked at her, surprised.

---

[14] Your first try at anything is always painful to remember. Anything you have never tried seems easy. Other people might tell you that it is difficult, but until you give it a shot yourself you never believe them. My throw at the red bowl was so optimistic it was painful. I thought that I could win the prize with one magical throw. It reminds me of Cynthia Lefcoe, the first woman I ever really loved. We met at the University of Guelph. Cynthia sat next to me in ENG 332Y. One day, I borrowed a pen from her and asked if she would like to see a movie that night. She had long red hair, and spoke in a soft voice that never seemed able to raise itself above an insistent whisper. Like me, she would be graduating in the spring. We went on a few dates, and then, even before we realized what was happening, we found ourselves in love. Some nights after we made love she would cry. I never asked her why. I knew that she was thinking about the future. Soon the letters of acceptance began to arrive. I got into the teaching program at the U of T, and she decided to do her graduate work at UBC. For the summer, we got a small apartment and moved in together. That summer was perfect. We didn't have to work, we didn't have to think; life was uncomplicated.

Eventually, September came and we had to go our separate ways. We wrote long letters to each other, and there were a few tearful long-distance phone calls, but soon we drifted apart. Today, Cynthia is the editor of a small literary magazine called *The Paper's Edge* and is married to a Vancouver lawyer.

I don't like to remember that summer. She was going to be a poet, and I was going to be the Great Canadian Novelist. "I'll be a high-school teacher only for a little while," I told her.

We promised each other that after we got our degrees and made some money we would move to Paris and live in squalor, just like Henry and June. Our love was like any first try; it was full of self-confidence, hope, and folly.

[15] My second try was different because I thought I knew what I was doing. It was like when I met my wife. I had just graduated from teachers college. I was teaching grade nine English at Bathurst Heights High School. I had a good salary, but was still living in the same small, cheap apartment that I had occupied as a student. Two years had passed since my breakup with Cynthia. One weekend, an old friend called and invited me to go on a double date with him. I didn't want to go, but he insisted. My date that night was a petite, dark woman named Maria Perry (now my ex). During the date, the other couple got into a fight and went home early. Neither Maria nor I wanted to be alone on a Friday, so we went out for coffee. At the time, she was working in a small art supply store, but she wanted to be a publicist. She was making some good contacts and was hoping to go into business for herself. A week later, we went out again, and in

I took my last ping-pong ball into my hand,[16] and decided to trust the winds of chance.

I closed my eyes and threw the ball straight up, in the general direction of the pyramid of fishbowls. It fell into one of the bowls filled with green water and a fish.

"We got a winner!" announced the man who ran the game. "You won!" Diane yelled.

"A winner! A winner! A winner!" screamed the carnie again, this time into a megaphone. People walking by looked at me and smiled. Then he handed me my prize in a dirty plastic bag. It was a goldfish.

"See you later," said the man. "Have a good time with the fish."

---

a year we were married. When I was offered a better paying job in the suburbs just north of Toronto, we moved out of my apartment and bought a house. We lived there for seven years. Those were very good years. I settled into my job and Maria was having increasing success as a publicist. I even finished a few chapters of the novel I had always said I would write. It would be called *The Quiet Painter*. The painter is very poor, but the small room in which he sleeps, eats, and paints, does not bother him. His friends – men who have become doctors, lawyers, and teachers – try to convince him to take a more practical approach to life. He refuses, and goes on painting. One day he meets a slim dancer with auburn hair and falls in love with her. She is more beautiful than any woman he has ever imagined. At first, he cannot bring himself even to touch her. But when he does, a terrible thing happens. He thinks that something has happened to his fingers. It seems as if his hands have a mind of their own. Soon it is apparent that he has become obsessed with her, and he cannot paint anything but portraits of her.

That was as far as I got. At the time, I didn't know how to end it. I didn't have anything left to say.

The years I spent with Maria were very good. We loved our jobs, we loved our life and we loved each other. But one day it all ended. Maria began to spend more time at the gallery. She never answered any of my questions. I was angry and confused and hurt. I didn't know what was happening. I felt betrayed. Then one night, the phone rang, and Maria informed me that she would not be coming home. She would drop by next week to pick up her things. She was in love with someone else. She was filing for divorce. I got the papers in the mail. Even when you think you understand the way things work, your second try is little better than your first.

[16] I could pay a dollar and try again, but then it might seem like I was trying too hard to win. The most important thing about winning is not looking like you care. I just closed my eyes and threw the last ball into the air because I understood that there was nothing I could do that would make any difference. If something is going to happen, it will happen, regardless of anything we do. One person cannot choose to stop loving another person any more than a star can decide to become a supernova. The secret is knowing when to close your eyes.